AUDITION

ALSO BY KATIE KITAMURA

Intimacies

A Separation

AUDITION

Katie Kitamura

RIVERHEAD BOOKS
NEW YORK
2025

RIVERHEAD BOOKS
An imprint of Penguin Random House LLC
1745 Broadway, New York, NY 10019
penguinrandomhouse.com

Copyright © 2025 by Katie Kitamura
Penguin Random House values and supports copyright. Copyright fuels creativity,
encourages diverse voices, promotes free speech, and creates a vibrant culture.
Thank you for buying an authorized edition of this book and for complying with
copyright laws by not reproducing, scanning, or distributing any part of it in
any form without permission. You are supporting writers and allowing
Penguin Random House to continue to publish books for every reader.
Please note that no part of this book may be used or reproduced in any manner
for the purpose of training artificial intelligence technologies or systems.

Riverhead and the R colophon are registered trademarks
of Penguin Random House LLC.

Library of Congress Cataloging-in-Publication Data

Names: Kitamura, Katie M., author.
Title: Audition / Katie Kitamura.
Description: New York : Riverhead Books, 2025.
Identifiers: LCCN 2024042072 (print) | LCCN 2024042073 (ebook) |
ISBN 9780593852323 (hardcover) | ISBN 9781101547892 (ebook)
Subjects: LCGFT: Novels.
Classification: LCC PS3611.I877 A93 2025 (print) |
LCC PS3611.I877 (ebook) | DDC 813/.6—dc23/eng/20240916
LC record available at https://lccn.loc.gov/2024042072
LC ebook record available at https://lccn.loc.gov/2024042073

First Riverhead hardcover edition: April 2025
International trade paperback edition ISBN: 9798217045839

Printed in the United States of America
3rd Printing

BOOK DESIGN BY MEIGHAN CAVANAUGH

The authorized representative in the EU for product safety and compliance is
Penguin Random House Ireland, Morrison Chambers, 32 Nassau Street,
Dublin D02 YH68, Ireland, https://eu-contact.penguin.ie.

PART I

1

IT SEEMED AN UNLIKELY CHOICE, THIS LARGE ESTABLISH-
ment in the financial district, so that I stood outside and
checked the address, the name of the restaurant, I wondered
if I had made a mistake. But then I saw him through the
window, seated at a table toward the back of the dining
room. I stared through the layers of glass and reflection, the
frame of my own face. Something uncoiled in my stomach,
slow and languorous, and I decided it would be better if I
left now, and did not go in to him.

At that moment, the front door opened and a man stepped
out, he inclined his head and held the door open, and because of that small courtesy—an invitation or injunction to

enter—I went inside. The foyer was busy with diners col-
lecting their coats, people surging in and then out of the
entryway, and briefly I allowed myself to be buffeted by
their movement. When the crowd dispersed, I could see
across the dining room floor again, he was bent over the
menu, examining it in a nervous posture. His table was between the entrance to the kitchen and the bathrooms, caught
in a stream of constant traffic. A pair of businessmen bumped
against its edge and he sat back impatiently, I saw him take a
deep breath, as if trying to collect or steady his thoughts.

The host asked if I had a reservation. I said that I was
meeting someone and indicated the young man seated at the
back of the restaurant. Xavier. It occurred to me that the
host must have been the person to seat him at this inhospitable table, and I saw a flicker of surprise cross his features
as I pointed. He looked quickly from my face to my coat to
my jewelry. It was my age, above all. That was the thing
that confounded him. He gave a tight smile and asked me
to please follow him. I was under no obligation to obey, I
could tell the host that I had made a mistake, or that something had come up, I could turn and slip away. But by that
point it seemed too late, and much as I had entered at the
behest of the man at the door, according to the imperative
of mere courtesy, I followed the host through the warren of
tables, each one occupied. I wondered again why Xavier had

chosen such a crowded venue at such a busy time, when we might just as easily have met elsewhere, in the afternoon, in the morning or early evening, for a coffee or quiet drink. The din pressed against me, crowding the inside of my head so that it was hard to think, difficult to locate my thoughts amidst the noise.

Xavier looked up as we approached. He set the menu down and rose to his feet, I remembered that he was unusually tall. I was momentarily intimidated, whether by him or by the situation I wasn't sure. He smiled and said that he hadn't been sure if I would come, he had been on the verge of giving up hope when at last he had seen me.

The host had already disappeared. We sat, one on either side of the table, me with my back to the wall. I looked across at Xavier and slowly unwound the scarf from my neck. He was still smiling, from the start I had noted his natural charm, his charisma. But I now saw that he dispensed it with too free a hand. He didn't seem to understand the intensity of its effect, or the fact that he moved through a world inhabited by other people. In this sense especially, he was still very young.

I put the scarf down and apologized and told him that I was usually on time. He shook his head, manner too eager, he said that there was no need to apologize, it was only because he was anxious, it was only because he'd been afraid that I would change my mind that he'd had such thoughts, under ordinary circumstances a five-minute delay would pass unnoticed, he was himself often late.

There was an awkward pause and then we both spoke at once—I asked how his classes were and he apologized for how he had behaved the last time we met. I understand how I must have sounded, he said. You must have wondered if I had lost my mind, if you had reason to worry. His words drowned out my question, the shore of ordinary conversation rapidly receding. He had spoken over me—not out of any chauvinism, I didn't think, but out of an excess of enthusiasm or nerves, he spoke like a person who did not have time to waste.

I looked at the menu and said that we should order, I wanted to eat and I wanted to have a drink, as soon as possible. He paused, then ducked his head down to examine the menu again. I asked if he already knew what he wanted and he said he wasn't especially hungry. I have no appetite, is what he said. Still, when the waiter arrived he asked for a hamburger and French fries, the order of a child. Despite myself, I smiled. I ordered my food and then asked the waiter to bring me a vodka tonic, it was past noon and I saw no reason not to start drinking.

As soon as the waiter left I looked at Xavier and asked again how his classes were. I was determined to put things on a more neutral footing, but in doing so I seemed to antagonize him, I could see that he took this dispassion as an affront. He was silent and then said in a sullen voice that his classes were fine. Fine, he said and nothing further. I pressed on, I asked who his professors were, it was possible I knew some of them, but he shook his head and said that he was mostly taking technical classes this semester, and that I was unlikely to know his instructors.

Still, I persisted. I'm interested to know what you are learning, I said. What kind of work you want to make. Who you admire.

I admire Murata, he said after a sly pause. I love his work.

I nodded warily.

Of course, you knew him.

Very little. I worked with him only once, and briefly. He died not long after. And we did not speak the same language. I did my lines phonetically, we worked through interpreters. The interaction was somewhat circumscribed.

What was he like?

He was brilliant, I said slowly. I was aware that Xavier was watching me closely, with a hunger that sat too close to the surface. He was already very sick, I said. He tired easily and it was only through sheer force of will that he finished the production. None of us knew he had cancer.

Parts of Speech is a masterpiece.

Yes.

I watched it again recently. You were so young.

I was. And now look at me.

I heard a teasing note in my voice, perhaps because I was not comfortable talking about Murata and I wanted to direct Xavier's attention elsewhere. The flirtation was a habit, one that had quieted over the years as I grew older, but that could still at times awaken. It was an error on my part. Xavier quickly leaned forward, as if he sensed an opening. I sat back again. Like all women, I had once been expert at negotiating the balance between the demands of courtesy and the demands of expectation. Expectation, which I knew to be a debt that would at some point have to be paid, in one form or another.

Xavier now said in a low voice, I want you to know that I accept what you told me. He seemed about to reach for my hands before pressing his palms down on the table, remaining in this strange pose for too long, the posture at once abject and defensive. I knew almost nothing about the person sitting across from me, I felt my skin grow hot as I recalled the fervor with which he had spoken that day at the theater, the feeling of repulsion and excitement that had stirred inside me. I was used to people armed with tremendous will, I was frequently with people whose job consists of imposing their reality upon the world. But now, as he seemed to shrink into himself in a manner subdued and uncertain, I wondered if in the end he was not one of these people, and did not truly know what he wanted from me.

The waiter arrived with our food, and as he hovered above us Xavier reluctantly slid his hands from the table and into his lap. The waiter began setting our plates down, his gaze moving surreptitiously from me to the young man and back again. I raised my head and his gaze skittered away. Xavier began to eat. As I watched him, the movement of his mouth as he chewed, his sinuous throat, I felt an unexpected charge between us. Although he was a stranger to me, in so many respects unfathomable, I knew the details of the fantasy he had created, the castle he had built in his mind, he had shared its private architecture with me and that disclosure was a form of intimacy.

The waiter cleared his throat and asked if there was anything else he could bring us, anything we needed. Xavier had eaten a third of his hamburger while the waiter was arranging the side plates and garnishes. He swallowed and took a long drink of water. The waiter's face, with its careful neutrality, was like a mask. As I stared at him, I suddenly recalled an incident many years ago, when I was not even twenty, in a restaurant much like this one, but in Paris. I had met my father there and he had taken me to lunch, I was then a thin scrap of a drama school student and in his general worry about me he ordered a vast succession of dishes. Once the waiter had gone, he told me he had something special that he wished to give me, something he and my mother had seen in a shop in Rome.

I opened the box with a gasp of delight. It was an emerald necklace, beautiful and extravagant, and once he fastened it around my neck I embraced him. I had not realized until that moment how much I missed the regular company of my parents. Perhaps my reactions were in some ways secondhand or performed—the gasp of delight, for example—but the feeling they were designed to express was sincere, I have that necklace still and I think of my parents whenever I wear it. But I also think of something else, another version or interpretation of the scene that took place between my father and me at that restaurant in Paris, and while it did not contaminate my memory of that lunch—one of the last before my father died—it did represent to me the definitive end of my girlhood and the start of the long stretch of what is called womanhood, the end of which was only now in turn beginning to approach.

We had settled into our meal, at that expensive restaurant in Paris with our crisply aproned waiter bringing dish after dish, my father had ordered too much food. The waiter also refilled our wineglasses, and I noticed that my father was drinking a lot again, in the middle of the day. It was when he was refilling my father's glass that the waiter turned very slightly toward me and gave a salacious wink. I was startled, my father asked if anything was wrong. I looked at the waiter, whose face was so impassive I wondered if I had imagined it. Nothing, I said. It's nothing. But my impression of the waiter had changed, and for the remainder of the meal I found his attention increasingly oppressive, the way he seemed to come too close when he set a dish before me, or swept the crumbs from the table, his manner full of an intimation that my father seemed not to notice, and that I noticed but did not fully understand. In and of itself, his flirtation was not so outrageous, he was not much older than I was and it was not as if I were immune to the attention of men. But it was only when my father had paid the rather substantial bill and we rose to go that I understood the precise nature of the insinuation the waiter had been making.

We were a few feet away from the table when I recalled the empty jewelry box I had left on the table and turned to retrieve it. As I reached for the box, the waiter appeared and pressed a piece of paper into my hand, which I immediately dropped in my confusion, but not before I saw that it was a telephone number, and not before the waiter had whispered in my ear, his breath hot and damp, Call me when you're done working. And I understood that he had mistaken my father and all his beautiful kindnesses to me that day for something else entirely. That was the first time I felt pity for my father, that he could be mistaken for a ludicrous and grasping old man, of the sort that needed to pay for company, of the sort with needs that could not freely be met.

And now, I thought I saw the same assessment in the eyes of the waiter, as he looked at me and then at the beautiful young man sitting opposite me. The shoe was on the other foot, I was now the object of pity, if not outright scorn—I was a woman, after all, and for women the judgment is always harsher. Curtly, I asked the waiter if I could have another drink and he nodded and whisked the empty glass away. As he departed, I met the gaze of a man seated several tables away. For a moment we stared at each other. Then he reached out and patted the hand of the woman sitting beside him, the gesture bloodless and reassuring. I understood well enough what the middle-aged couple believed was taking place between us, and I felt a wave of irritation, and then also a feeling of sympathy for Xavier, I remembered what it was like to be so young, and to be seen always in relation to the fulfillment of an older person's desires.

Do you enjoy living in the city? I asked abruptly.

He set his fork and knife down and wiped his mouth with his napkin, he had very good table manners, he had been nicely brought up. He was what used to be called presentable, a young man who did not lack for money or care. Yes, he said. I love it here, I would do anything to stay. He spoke with ease, and also with the expectation that this, the desired outcome, would come to pass. I understood that he was in essence a confident person, my first impression of him had been the correct one. The young man who had appeared in the doorway of the theater, his body only a little tense. I remembered that Lou had immediately risen to her feet to go and ask what he wanted, if she could help, I remembered turning and seeing how she smiled up at him, and how he smiled in return.

It was my presence that turned him inward, that changed the composition of his personality. I knew then that I had been wrong to come. I had a natural inclination to press my face against the glass, to peer at the mystery of other people, but I also had an instinct for self-preservation. I knew how to draw the lines firmly and rapidly when necessary, how to pull down the shutter and withdraw. I had not touched my fish but Xavier had eaten, now was the time to speak decisively.

I don't think we should see each other again, I said once the waiter had taken our plates away. Xavier flinched, as if I had struck him. No relationship between us can be possible.

Everything you said to me—I accept it. I understand. I really do.

Then why did you want to meet?

He hesitated. There's something I need to tell you.

The man at the nearby table was observing us again, I could feel his eyes on me and I looked up in irritation. But what I saw past him caused me to stop in confusion. I saw Tomas enter the restaurant, although this was not possible, he had told me that very morning that he would be at home working the entire day, he was never in this part of town and had no reason to be at a restaurant like this, which he would have hated. It must have started raining, he carried an umbrella and carefully shook the water off it as he entered, his movements deliberate, as they always were. He spoke to the host, who nodded and indicated the rapidly emptying dining room, probably telling him he had his pick of the tables.

I'll be right back, Xavier said and began to rise to his full height.

No, I said. Sit down.

I had spoken more sharply than I intended. He sat down. He was staring at me, perhaps it was the first time I had genuinely taken him by surprise. Tomas was now following the host into the dining room. I wondered what the best course of action was, whether I should simply catch his eye, wave from across the restaurant. That would be the natural thing to do, I could say that Xavier was a student, which he was, a young person interested in the theater. But then Tomas would join us, that would also only be natural, and from there an entire cascade of events would follow. Xavier was looking at me strangely. Is anything wrong? he asked. Tomas was now halfway across the restaurant and I was preparing to stand, to bluff my way through the situation as best I could. He had not yet seen me but it would not be long, there were perhaps a dozen occupied tables, the host was walking rapidly in our direction, it was only a question of time. Tomas was following, his manner a little vague and distracted, as if his mind were elsewhere. I watched from across the restaurant, he appeared so much older from a distance and I felt a pang of tenderness, of love, in that moment I could not understand why I had not told him about Xavier, when I told him everything, when I trusted him more than any person in the world.

Tomas would understand. Of course he would. It was with this thought in mind that I raised my hand, as if to get his attention. Sit down, I would say. Join us. This is—and I would introduce Xavier to Tomas, who would sit beside me. His presence would calm me, it would remove all threat from the situation. I waved my arm through the air, Tomas was only a dozen feet away, I was sure he must have seen us. Xavier turned, his face confused, his gaze swept across the room but did not linger on Tomas, whom he did not know and had never met. Xavier gave me a questioning look, I only raised my hand higher, signaling.

But at that moment, Tomas froze. He had his hands in his coat pockets and he began rummaging inside, as if looking for something—his phone or his wallet, perhaps his keys. He had stopped in the middle of the restaurant, I should have risen to my feet and gone to him, but I did not move. As I watched, Tomas spoke to the host, who nodded and shrugged. Tomas turned and retreated, walking swiftly across the dining room floor, as if he had forgotten or lost some item of importance. At the same time, alongside or propelling that urgency, was something shamefaced, something hidden and untoward.

The glass door opened and swung shut. I turned to watch as Tomas hurried away down the street. I felt, in his departure, a feeling of regret so pronounced it seemed to exert a gravitational pull, it seemed to pull me to the ground. I could have gotten to my feet and called him back. I could have run after him, tugged at his arm. But there had been something that stopped me. When had it last happened, that I had looked at my husband and seen an emotion or expression that I was not easily able to parse, the meaning of which was not apparent at first glance? Was he hiding something—the reason for his presence in this restaurant, which was in the wrong part of town, at the wrong time of day, particularly for a creature of such habit?

Is everything okay?

I turned to look at Xavier and then I saw it—the similarity between us, which was more than the fact of our shared race, it was an echo or mirroring in our features that had no explanation, no purpose. In that moment, I could perceive the outer edge of his thought, his personal delusion, I could almost reach out and grasp it. But then the feeling receded and the gap between us yawned once more. He sat back in his chair and exhaled and I recognized the movement, it was the one he had done at the theater, when we first met.

An old gesture of mine that he had lifted from my films, my stage performances, and copied without shame. A piece of me, on the body of a stranger, a thing of mine that had been taken and moved into the realm of the uncanny by this young man sitting across from me. Anger surged through me, a sharpening of all my instincts. The situation was more dangerous than I had previously understood, below the surface demands and obtrusions of his personality was a ruthlessness I had not perceived or prepared for. I need to go, I said to Xavier, and before he could reply I rose to my feet and stepped back from the table, I had nothing else to say, I could only repeat, I need to go.

2

I PUSHED OPEN THE FRONT DOOR OF THE RESTAURANT
and tumbled outside, I looked but there was no sign of
Tomas, he had disappeared into the densely populated street.
There was a rain so faint it was mist in the air. I thought of
Xavier, whom I had left at the table without explanation,
and I began walking quickly down the street, away from the
restaurant.

As I turned the corner and walked north, I breathed in
the cold air as if I had been long deprived of oxygen. It was
too far to walk back to the apartment in the rain but I could
not bear the thought of taking the subway or sitting in a car,
I needed to feel myself decisively moving away from the

situation inside the restaurant—Xavier sitting across from me at the table, Tomas standing frozen on the other side of the dining room. Now, as the rain grew heavier, I continued to walk as if to chastise myself, I couldn't understand why I had agreed to meet Xavier in the first place.

I had felt sorry for him perhaps—to have so much unreciprocated feeling, to be carrying that imbalance. But had it only been that? Hadn't there also been some underlying curiosity, an old instinct to draw close to other people? When I was younger, that impulse had almost been the governing principle of my life. I had tried many times to explain this compulsion to myself—it was a way of being in the world, of relating to the life that was taking place around me, it was a question of being open. But over the years and in particular once I met Tomas, I had learned to curtail that urge, to see it for what it really was—a passing curiosity, a spirit of bedevilment, and a form of voyeurism.

Because of Tomas. Through him, with him, I had learned to live with greater discipline, to inhabit a certain quietude, so that I no longer fully remembered what it felt like to be so open to the world, to take such pleasure in throwing myself onto the crashing waves of other people's temperament. I had been surprised when the feeling had overtaken me once more and with no small urgency, I had been compelled by Xavier and his strange predicament, in all its wild illogic. I had become curious despite knowing better. The situation bore every red flag that I had learned to recognize over the years, and yet I had replied to his message, I had agreed to meet with him, I had gone into the restaurant and sat down across the table from him.

It had been a heedless moment. I had entered the stage of life where there is a certain amount of immutability, in middle age, change is experienced primarily as a kind of attrition. Perhaps for that reason I had been lulled into a state of unthinking complacency. As I continued walking down the street, through that soft rain, I began to wonder how long I had been in this state of excessive inurement. I looked around me, I saw that I had walked much further than I had thought, I was almost home.

When I returned to the apartment, Tomas was not there. We lived in the West Village, in an apartment we purchased not too long after I worked with Murata, on the film that Xavier had mentioned. That was my first taste of success, and although the role was small and the film in another language, it had achieved some renown. The parts began to come a little more regularly after that, although still circumscribed in scope and scale, none of them equal in depth to what Murata had offered me.

Mostly it meant that we had a bit more money, that I could pay the bills and buy the clothes I wanted, that we could eat out when we did not feel like cooking. In the years that followed, we began to accumulate a little money, there would be residuals here and there, a guest role on a television series. It helped that we did not have children. Children, with their mouths to feed, clothes to purchase, the cost of childcare and tuition, we had friends who informed us that one partner's entire salary went toward paying for the nanny. In this way, although we were by no means wealthy, we found ourselves in the unexpected position of being what is referred to as *comfortable*—no small feat, in a city like New York.

We purchased the apartment, all those years ago—although not so many as someone newer to the city might think, the churn of gentrification moved with extraordinary speed—and we had a reasonable mortgage. With two bedrooms and a study for Tomas, the apartment was large enough for us to grow old in. You might think that people wondered how we did it, a sizable apartment in the West Village, considering the sporadic nature of our employment. But the truth is that almost nothing about the way people live in New York makes any sense, least of all when it comes to money. Probably they assumed we had some private income, or perhaps, after I had achieved some further success, they imagined that I was better and more regularly paid than I was. Certainly, as we grew older and more established in life, people ceased to enter the apartment with an expression of mild surprise. The place came to seem more natural. We grew into it, and then we never outgrew it.

That afternoon, though, the air in the apartment was stale and I felt as if I were entering a space long uninhabited, for a brief moment it was as if I had come into an apartment that looked exactly like my home in every last particular, down to the vase on the table in the hall and the coats hanging from the rack, and yet was not my home at all. I called out to Tomas. It was late afternoon, the hour when his working day would usually come to a conclusion and he would emerge from his office in search of a drink. The start to the evening, the time when I would join him if I was not working, and we would talk a little before proceeding with our plans for the night, sometimes there was an event or social obligation, sometimes it was only a quiet dinner, but either way, always the calm of each other's company.

But that day his office was empty, and as I made my way down the corridor I saw that the door had been left ajar, so that I could peer inside at the empty desk and the chair asunder, the monitor of his computer black with inactivity. The room was tidy, there was no sign of his presence—no indication that he had merely stepped out to get something from the corner shop, or to drop off a package at the post office. I returned to the kitchen, which was pristine, there were no dishes in the sink or crumbs on the counter. On a normal day there would be a collection of dirty coffee cups and plates, the crusts of sandwiches, the debris of a productive day. I stood in the kitchen and stared at the immaculate surface of the counter, it was only then that I realized how much I experienced those objects as evidence of the hard-won consistency of our life together.

That morning, I had asked him what his plans were for the day. Nothing planned, a clear day to write, he said he would be home working. I asked what he would do for lunch and he said he would make do with what was in the kitchen. If I had not seen him at the restaurant, I would have likely called or sent him a message, I would have asked where he was and if everything was okay. I frowned and left the kitchen, it had been a long time since I had wondered where Tomas was, or how he was spending his time. Even when he was traveling for work—or indeed when I was, it was not as if we were together at all times, there could be weeks or even months when we did not see each other, and yet during all those times, I never wondered what he was doing.

I sat down in the living room, the light outside was rapidly fading. If my imagination had atrophied from lack of use, it now returned with surprising force, it took only a few small things—an empty sink, the polished surface of a counter, an unexpected appearance in a restaurant—for uncertainty to breed, for speculation to return. I blinked in the growing dark. I had been unnerved to see Tomas at the restaurant, not only because of my own transgression—that was the moment when I understood that Xavier was a secret, something I had chosen not to share with Tomas, although I didn't know why—but because he had seemed like someone who had secrets of his own.

Was such a thing possible? Tomas was still a handsome man, if anything he had become better looking over the years, the rough edges of his youth rubbed smooth. When he was younger there had been something grasping in his manner, which was not unusual in someone so ambitious, someone who wished to make his mark upon the world and who cared what people thought of him. But as he attained further success in his work, he became less interested in what other people thought, his ego no longer requiring external reinforcement, and then less interested in other people more generally.

Some part of that, I knew, was due to the happiness of our marriage. But that settled affect also scanned as confidence, and confidence can be a large part of what a woman finds attractive in a man. Perhaps, for some women, it was even the main thing. Tomas was, or so I believed, largely indifferent to other women, I had been with him at parties and gatherings where there had been a number of remarkably beautiful women, whom he seemed hardly to notice. But could that genuinely be possible? Did he really move through the world so blinkered? The notion, its blithe confidence, now seemed ludicrous and naïve.

Restless, I stood up and turned on the lights. It was past seven and still no word from Tomas. I had a sudden vision of his face, the slow stirring of interest in his features, striking in a man typically so aloof. It was a version of my husband I never knew. When Tomas and I met he had been different, everything had been outwardly directed, he had been seeking things from the world. I suppose one of those things was me. Now he had those things and he was another man altogether, and this version of him—this duplicitous person I was imagining—was a stranger to me, or nearly, it was like recalling someone I had briefly met long ago, in another life and country.

Then the door opened and he came in, the same Tomas as always. He hung up his coat and hat on the rack, he looked over to me in the living room and he smiled, the familiar lines appearing at his eyes. I felt immediate relief at the mere sight of him, the fever breaking, and I chided myself for my fears. He came into the room and leaned over and kissed me, I'm sorry I'm late, he said. He backed away and went into the kitchen. Do you want another drink? he said over his shoulder. I looked to the side table where my glass was sitting, I had forgotten that I had poured a drink, forgotten that I had finished it, but Tomas noticed everything. I turned, he was already in the kitchen. Where were you? I called out after him as I rested my hand on the glass.

The pause that followed was so infinitesimal that it might have been imagined, or it might have been merely the product of some minor circumstance—ice sticking to the tray, an unyielding stopper, a speck of dust in the eye. It might have been, and yet my senses were roused again and I sat up as he came back into the living room cradling his drink in one hand, exactly as he always did, but perhaps too exactly, and said, I forgot that I was having lunch with Said. We went to his studio after, he had some new work that he wanted to show me, and then we got to talking. Tomas sat down in the chair opposite mine, his favorite chair. I stared at him and he smiled in his friendly way.

Do you know, it's been over two years since we've seen Said?

We went to his opening last year.

I know, but really seen him.

We don't see as many people as we might.

He nodded and took a sip from his glass.

What was the work like?

He lifted his head, startled.

What work?

Said's new paintings.

You know, I think it's because of his girlfriend, he said ruminatively. She's so irritating. Said really did mess things up with Raphaelle, I mean he's terrible with women.

Yes, I know. But never mind about his love life—we had known Said for many years and it was always the same thing, too dull to relate much less live through, I didn't know how he did it—how is the new work?

Said had a successful gallery career that was predicated on small shifts in his practice, sufficiently minute that his market remained untroubled, but together substantial enough to create the impression of artistic evolution. Lately however, Said had talked of making larger changes in his work, he was tired of pandering to the market, even if it had made him enormously wealthy. I wondered what he had done, what that work might look like, it was not always easy to do something new after so many years of doing the same thing, however talented you might be. And Said was a talented artist, notwithstanding his commercial success, we had a small canvas hanging in the living room, a gift for some wedding anniversary or another, a tribute to the marital success that we had and that he had yet to attain, or so he had put it when he presented it to us.

I therefore asked the question out of genuine curiosity, and it was only when Tomas continued to stare at me vacantly that suspicion began to grow in me again, blooming with rude health. I saw the panic that he was not entirely able to conceal, and that was so unusual that I felt anxiety prickle through to the surface of my skin, newly acute.

I really don't know what to say about it, he said. He was flushed and he shook his head. It's terrible. All this time, we've been encouraging him to do something new, to break out of this, this—rut that we felt he was in.

But what has he done? What are the paintings like? I persisted.

He shook his head again, I had the feeling he was deflecting, I could almost see him inventing a plausible body of work in his head, the more I thought about it the more unlikely it seemed that Said had made any real change in the direction of his work, he was extremely talented, but he was also lazy and comfortable and too used to the cocoon of praise and money in which he lived. What was more surprising was the fact that Tomas, who was expert at constructing stories, had chosen to fabricate one that was so transparent, so hastily thrown together.

They were abstract. Shapes and colors.

Shapes and colors? I repeated.

He didn't look at me, but stood up and walked back into the kitchen. *Shapes and colors* is not so unusual a description, but it was for Tomas, who generally spoke with precision, so that his words called forth sharply delineated images and ideas, I had never heard him describe a painting as *shapes and colors*. I frowned and followed him into the kitchen. Is everything okay, I asked. You seem—

I seem what?

His voice was blunt and I took an involuntary step back. Was there a twinge of reproach in his face? He held out a drink and asked, And how was your day? What did you get up to? He took a sip, eyes level with mine over the rim of his glass.

Fine?

Just fine? With a question mark?

I stared at him. What was he playing at? If he had seen me, why didn't he simply ask? We did not fight often, we were not a couple who thrived on confrontation, but we were more than capable of having an argument if necessary. Or so I had always thought, suddenly I was no longer certain. His face was difficult to read, as I looked his features seemed to soften with vulnerability and I turned away in shame. But when I looked back it was as if a defensive carapace had slid into place, his face again expressionless.

He set down his glass and carefully picked an olive from a bowl he must have filled, there were small bowls of olives and also nuts on the counter and now he said that he was very hungry. I've hardly eaten all day, he said and smoothly continued, as if to forestall my question, Said wanted to eat at a place in the financial district, one of those restaurants where each dish is so tiny that at the end of the meal you're still hungry. He continued to cram nuts into his mouth and I thought that he must really have been hungry, he ate with a gusto that was not in and of itself off-putting, it was simply a man eating, and yet I recoiled, something in the crunching movement of his jaw was alien, it was briefly the face of someone who thought he was alone. I haven't been to that part of town in years, he said. It was strange to be there. What an inhospitable neighborhood, I have no idea why Said chose a restaurant there, although I think he owns a part of it, I'm not sure, it was hard to tell.

His voice was now completely natural. He turned to me and smiled and murmured, Come here, and I went to him. He embraced me, his arms tight against my shoulders, and when he released me he said, again in a voice that was perfectly, seamlessly natural, This restaurant of Said's was oddly interchangeable with all the restaurants in that neighbor-hood, it even had one of those names that sound like all the other names, heavy in vowels—Aita, Elea, Amane—I walked into another restaurant and was about to sit down before I realized I was in the wrong place. But it was full, if Said invested in it he will have done well with his money.

I nodded, as I listened to him I felt myself finally begin-ning to relax, the explanation for his brief appearance at the restaurant was perfectly coherent, it was true that the name of the restaurant was brief and full of vowels, true that it looked like every other restaurant in the neighborhood, it was an easy mistake to make. And Said was always invest-ing his money in one scheme or another, I remembered, even if Tomas had not, that he had purchased a share in a new restaurant several years ago, a venture that had presumably reached fruition, so that he was now able to meet his friends for lunch at his restaurant, nothing in the world could be more like Said.

Reassured, almost giddy with relief, I laughed and asked what we should do about dinner. It's too late to cook, shall we go out? I placed my hands on his face, he kissed them and smiled and appeared entirely himself. It occurred to me that it had been a long time since we had looked at each other so closely, since I had regarded his face with such scru-tiny and attention. I continued to gaze at Tomas, long enough that he asked if everything was okay. I said it was nothing, only that I loved him. He kissed me and asked if we should just go to the restaurant on the corner, it was the easiest thing. I nodded, I said to give me ten minutes and I would be ready to go.

I went into the bathroom and splashed some water on my face. I was sweating, the heat was always too high in the apartment during the winter, no matter how many calls we made to the building management. I stripped off my sweater and stood before the mirror, my skin was strangely mottled, my appearance repulsive. More and more often, I was surprised by the person in the mirror, it was not the lines at my mouth or the hollowness around my eyes, it was the lag in recognition that was the most troubling, the brief moment when I looked in the mirror and did not know who I was. I changed and fixed my makeup and returned to the living room. Tomas was sitting in his favorite armchair with another drink, it occurred to me that we were on our way to becoming alcoholics. I asked if he was ready to go and he grunted and drained his glass before rising to his feet.

At the door, as I pulled my coat on, he came forward and helped wind the scarf around my neck, the same scarf I had worn to lunch with Xavier, and which Tomas had bought for me on a whim, on a trip we had taken to London. I turned to face him, his hand lingered and then tightened on the scarf, as if he were recalling that day—as if the memory had been imbued with extra meaning, although I could not think what that meaning might be, I remembered little about the trip. I looked at him in surprise, and he said very quietly, You're not cheating on me again, are you? No, I whispered at once, and I was a little frightened as I said it. He nodded and said, Forget I mentioned it, and opened the door for me and we stepped out.

3

I NOW KNEW BEYOND DOUBT THAT TOMAS HAD SEEN me at the restaurant, that this was the reason he had suddenly departed, and that he had done so because he thought, or worried, or wondered if what he was seeing was evidence of infidelity. But I didn't know how to interpret the manner in which he had asked the question, both direct and distressingly oblique, arriving as it did without context or explanation, and abandoned without any further interrogation or demand for reassurance. Why hadn't he come up to us at the restaurant, asked who Xavier was and why we were together? Had he looked at me and understood that I did not want to be seen, had the meaning of that scene—the two of us, sharing a meal—then become at once too obvious and too painful to address?

In walking away, had he in fact been attempting to forestall the conclusion that seemed, even at a glance, all too clear? The mind—even a mind as sharp and particular as the one belonging to Tomas—reaches for the most obvious explanation, and in the way of Occam's razor, the most obvious explanation is often also the correct one. I knew that what Tomas—what the waiter, and the middle-aged couple sitting at the nearby table, what they had all been misled by was the current of intensity running between Xavier and me.

Its source was an imbalance of want. Two people who want the same thing will never generate the same intensity as two people who want different things, or one person who wants into an absence, a void—as was in fact the case with Xavier, who wanted something from me that I could not give. More than that—he wanted something that I could not begin to fathom, a desire with which it felt dangerous to collude or to involve myself. Yes, there had been conflict in the air between us, conflict and intensity, and that had read as carnal interest, because the actual story, the reality of what was happening between us in that moment, was much less easily imagined.

After that day in the restaurant, things were never entirely the same between Tomas and me. It wasn't a façade or a pretense that suddenly fell away—our marriage was much more than mere surface or appearance—it was the substance of our relationship itself, guarded by a shared reality, that changed. You pull at the ropes tied to the statue, you pull and nothing happens, and then you pull and you pull again and the whole thing topples over.

What actually happened is this. Two weeks before I met Xavier for lunch, I was at the theater. I was sitting in the house watching Josie and Clarice rehearse, it was a complex scene and they had been working for some time already. I remember watching them in a state of heightened attention, as they picked through the scene and analyzed the individual pieces, until the totality began to emerge and it was like a small miracle was taking place in the room. I began to forget that time was passing, the world outside. Toward the end of the rehearsal, just before Anne called for a break, I became aware of a young man standing in the aisle at the back, observing.

That was the first time I saw Xavier. He had a striking appearance and for that reason I assumed he was there to meet with Anne, perhaps a general meeting or perhaps something more formal for a part. Lou immediately stood and went to him, and I remember thinking that even if he was without talent he would enjoy some level of success, in some capacity, he had a face that was made for being looked at.

Although he also seemed awkward and even shy, when he saw me looking at him he visibly started.

I sat back into my seat and my attention returned to Josie and Clarice. I was instantly engaged in the intricacies of their rehearsal, as if my focus had never shifted, I had worked with both of them but I did not think they had previously worked together. I could see that they were strongly attracted to each other, in their mutual admiration, their curiosity, but at the same time there was an edge of rivalry between them that had the potential to flare into open antagonism, it was the nature of the work and its rapid, temporary intimacies. And so, in addition to the story of the play itself, the narrative that was being enacted by Josie and Clarice, I was also observing the drama between the two women, who at times circled each other in the manner of prizefighters, wary and in a posture of constant assessment.

There are always two stories taking place at once, the narrative inside the play and the narrative around it, and the boundary between the two is more porous than you might think, that is both the danger and the excitement of the performance. The air becomes thin, the senses keener, there is too much reverberation. I was remembering all the times that I had been in that precise situation, and was therefore thoroughly absorbed as I watched the rehearsal, in a state of almost preternatural concentration, which was suddenly broken when Anne's assistant, Lou, touched my arm. At that same moment Anne called for a break and the energy in the room dissipated, the attention scattering.

He's here to see you.

She indicated Xavier. Me? I asked, and I stood up, curious. I walked over to him and he immediately came forward and introduced himself. I took his hand a little confusedly, he said that he was very happy to be meeting me, and then added that the situation was a little strange. I didn't know what he meant but I nodded, and asked how I could help. I had reverted to the most distant version of myself, the version that sounded like a bank manager or hotel concierge, I was puzzled by his presence, I didn't know who he was or why he was here or how he even came to know I was at the theater that day. Then Xavier said that what he had to tell me was complicated, complicated but important. He paused, he said he was making a terrible mess of it. But he wondered if I would have a coffee with him. Now. During the break. It was—he looked in the direction of Anne, who seemed to be observing us, and I wondered if she knew the young man, if that was the connection—she had said thirty minutes? We could go out to the lobby, to the café there.

I could see Josie and Clarice looking toward me from opposite sides of the theater, both wearing expressions of anguish and determination, and I knew that each would want to discuss the other with me, perhaps in order to ask for advice but mostly in order to vent their worry and frustration. I saw Josie get to her feet and I decided it would be better to bypass that particular situation and its attendant complexities, I didn't want to be drawn in to either side, and so I said, Yes, let's go now. I could see the surprise on Xavier's face—I realized then that he had not expected me to say yes—and even a little apprehension, as if he were suddenly not sure that he really wanted to say whatever it was he had come here to say. Over his shoulder, I could see that Josie was now raising a hand, as if to get my attention, and quickly I hooked Xavier under the elbow and steered him back down the aisle and through the exit.

The soft sucking sound of the double doors closing. Although it had not been loud inside the theater, as we stood in the lobby it felt newly quiet. Is the café open? I asked and he nodded. Fine, I said, let's go. We were silent as we moved across the densely carpeted lobby, our footsteps muffled so that we made no sound, it was as if we had entered another world. I told Xavier to sit down and went to the counter to order our coffees. As I waited for the woman to make the drinks, I observed the young man. He was sitting at a table by the window, his posture a little hunched and his face stretched tight with tension. In this full light, I saw that my first impression had been correct, he was handsome, perhaps even excessively so—his face would breed the kind of desire that would turn upon itself, too much to be useful to him, I had known such men and women.

I took our coffees and sat down across the table from him. He looked at me and to my surprise I saw in him a sudden avarice. I became immediately wary, probably he thought I would be able to help him get a job, perhaps he wanted me to petition Anne on his behalf, I had the definite sensation that he would now try to manipulate me. I almost laughed. He was young and had probably made his way through life seducing everyone around him, from his mother and father to his teachers and babysitters, a habit formed early in life. I fell regrettably in between roles, neither young enough to be romantic quarry nor prone to any maternal feeling.

Of course, as it turned out, I was the only one who believed this to be true. It was altogether possible that a woman of forty-nine would fall in love with a young man of twenty-five, and it was even possible that a young man of twenty-five would fall in love with a woman of forty-nine. Perhaps I knew this to be the case, without wanting to acknowledge it, perhaps that was why I was so swift to reject the narrative that even then seemed to occur to both of us. I found myself on guard, and as if aware of this, he appeared to change tack. Leaning back into his chair, he said that what he was going to tell me would sound as if it made no sense, and that he apologized in advance for presenting it so baldly, but in the end there was no other way of doing it, he had very good reason to believe that we were related.

I stared at him blankly. How?

I think you might be my mother.

I genuinely thought I had misheard him. Then I laughed, in an outburst of astonishment. I'm so sorry, I said, but that's not possible.

Please, he said. And there was a bright intensity to his eyes that briefly silenced me, so that he was able to continue. My parents have told me some things about my birth mother. Not a lot, but certain details—about where my mother was born, where she went to school, her line of work.

Yes, but—

I laughed again in disbelief.

And then I read a profile of you, he continued, and you talked about giving up a child, some time ago. I stared at him uneasily, I knew at once what he was referring to, it was an interview I had given years earlier, in which I had referred to an abortion I'd had, long before my marriage to Tomas. I had been troubled by the silence that had constellated around the abortion, as if it were a subject not to be mentioned or discussed in polite company, when I told people they fell silent or changed the subject, so that I had the impression I'd told them something they would rather not have known.

Their discomfort only escalated when my then partner was present, they behaved as if perhaps they should offer condolences, then seemed to realize how absurd the impulse was and ended up staring into the middle distance between us, so that I had the unpleasant sensation that they were seeing the specter of some unborn child, hovering in the air above our shoulders. There were their conscious principles and then there was their instinctual response, which was for the subject to remain abstract and above all private, and it was this second response that I encountered, again and again, in different contexts and even as the years continued to pass.

Perhaps for this reason, I had spoken openly about the abortion in the interview, I suppose I had been foolish enough to think it would make a difference for me to share this information. The young journalist listened to me closely and with what I thought was great sympathy, she agreed that it was a pity, the shadow still associated with abortion, despite everything, even the word was not used as frequently as it might be. And it mattered, the vocabulary, the way a word circulated through society, the context and atmosphere that was created around it.

But in the piece she wrote, she not only failed to use the word *abortion*, she used language that was confusing to say the least, that seemed designed to obfuscate the reality of the procedure that I'd had. Obfuscate, or perhaps erase—I knew well enough how the words *give up a child* might sound in certain quarters, how my experience might be retrofitted to suit a conservative fantasy of adoption, a living child out in the world. I let it go. I could have asked for a correction, but the language was vague and nobody—at least nobody I met, nobody I knew—seemed under the impression that I had given a child up for adoption, nobody that is until Xavier.

I stared at him now, the root of his misapprehension suddenly a little bit comprehensible, a little bit plausible, although not really, it remained insufficient, he was evidently in the grip of some serious delusion, or else he was a grifter of some kind, it was one or the other. He continued, And the dates and ages, they line up, so that became another thing. And I thought—here, a strange expression crossed his face, as if now at last he was casting his line—in the interview, that you expressed some regret about that choice.

He paused. I tried to remember what the journalist had written, no doubt she had attributed regret to this phantom decision, why would she not? It was only a feeling, an intuition, he continued, but you see, I thought I had nothing to lose. I thought, there's no harm in asking. He leaned forward. That was perhaps the first time I really saw his face, the first time I did more than merely look, and to my chagrin, it occurred to me that one of the reasons I had been so quick to consider him attractive was because of the essential similarity in our appearance. We were comparable in coloring, there was the question of race, perhaps there were even individual features that could be considered alike. It was a likeness, though one without the meaning he desired.

He sat back in his chair with a soft exhalation. It was a perfectly expressive movement—from the fluttering of the lips at the exhalation of air, the slight slump of the shoulders before the little wriggle back upright—although I did not know exactly what it meant. I felt a little pity for him. But then, as he leaned forward again, his expression both vulnerable and winning, a man used to getting his way, I realized with a growing sense of horror that I myself had made that exact gesture, had utilized it, to be more precise, many times in my work. There had even been a period when it had become something of a tic, a series of movements that I relied upon when I did not know how to work my way out of a scene, when I was uncertain of what was happening with a character at a particular moment, or when the writing was so thin that some weight needed to be affixed to the words in order to give them significance.

It was Tomas who had pointed it out to me, in his gentle but definite way, and although I denied it—I was perhaps even angry, nobody likes to be exposed in this way—I stopped at once. One of the benefits of my profession is that I have excellent control over my body, reserves of discipline that can be called upon. By that point however, the gesture had been committed to film in at least three or four different performances. It was not something that anyone else had noticed, no director had ever taken me aside and told me to stop, stop with the soft exhalations, stop with the downward movement of the shoulders and then the straightening of the spine (to indicate, of course, a gathering of spirit or energy, the entire thing was shamefully literal when you examined it closely).

I had a vision of this young man, watching all those old movies to find the precise moment of repetition, embarrassingly the context and scene and genre varied wildly and yet I had stubbornly used the same gesture, thinking about it further I had to admit there were probably many more than three or four instances, as I said, for a time it had been deeply ingrained in the little repertoire of movements and reactions that I unconsciously relied upon. I imagined him finding and isolating each of these moments, studying and recreating them in the mirror, honing the reproduction so that he might deploy it now, at this moment of confrontation. And I also realized why, at first, I had been uncertain of what the gesture meant—because it had been used in so many different contexts, it had grown threadbare and without meaning.

I scanned his face, which was perfectly neutral, as if he were not even aware of the little trick of impersonation he had just performed, and I no longer knew if it was conscious or not, if the gesture had simply crept from my body into his by way of repeated observation. And even if the mimicry was conscious, I did not know if he displayed it in order to prove to me that there was indeed a semblance between us, if he believed that I would feel at that moment some recognition, the source and mechanics of which I would somehow not apprehend. Was it that, or was it something else altogether? A gesture of intimidation, a way to show me that he knew me better than I realized, that he had burrowed unfathomably deep into the details of my life and my person. My cup was now lukewarm to the touch and I lowered my hand to my lap. My heart was beating rapidly. The most obvious explanation was that he was a con artist. For the first time, I understood the presence of the word *artist* in that moniker. If this was a con, there was a remarkable level of artistry to it, more than was strictly necessary, it was artistry for the sake of artistry alone. I looked at the clock behind the counter and rose to my feet, I said the break was nearly over and I needed to return to the theater. He too rose to his feet, and seemed about to follow me. I held up a hand, No, I said firmly. I saw the woman behind the counter look up. There's no need, I said. The journalist misunderstood. There was no child. What you're suggesting is an impossibility.

I backed away, hand extended, and then turned and

walked to the theater. For a moment I thought I heard his footsteps behind me, the grip of his hand on my arm, and I flinched. But I would not have heard his footsteps on the thick carpet, and there was no touch on my arm, there was only the force of my imagining. I opened the door to the theater and stepped inside. I stood for a moment, eyes adjusting to the dark, the fresh noise of the company. The sweet and musty odor. Outside, there was silence. I felt a little relief, to be away from the young man, and then a jolt of unforced admiration, for the totality of his performance. I barely knew what the performance was for, what form it took or what purpose it served, but I understood even then that it was a performance of the highest order.

Perhaps that was why, when Anne said a few days later that Xavier had been in touch and that she had given him my email, I did not say anything, did not even tell her that I wished she hadn't, and perhaps that was why when he sent an email asking if we could meet, against my better judgment, against even basic rationality, I agreed. I remember thinking, why not. I remember the strong impulse of my curiosity. I remember too, of course, his face. When I entered the theater and sat down, Anne came over, she asked who the young man was, and I hesitated and then I said—but why?—Oh, just a friend of the family.

4

THE WEEK AFTER I MET XAVIER FOR LUNCH WAS A PE-
riod of extraordinary concordance in my marriage, a period
I would later examine, one that I would remember. I had
not been so closely attuned to Tomas in years, to the subtle
weather of his moods, the cartography of his expression. It
would not be an exaggeration to say that I thrilled to his
presence, or that I had a new appreciation of his intelligence
and kindness. This was undoubtedly because, for the first
time in many years, I saw our marriage for what it really
was, something fragile that could still be tarnished or lost.
Tomas himself was almost exactly the same. He did not bring
up the question of infidelity again, and as the days crept by,

even as I retained this sense of hyperattunement, I began to wonder if I had attributed false meaning to his quiet question. He did not ask where I spent my days, as he'd had cause to in the past, or to whom I was speaking, he behaved as if nothing between us had changed.

Another week passed. We had breakfast together, as we always did, and I was getting ready to leave the apartment when Tomas suddenly said that he would join me, he wanted to get a little air and stretch his legs before he sat down to write. I said that I would like his company very much and he gave a small, distracted smile. As he pulled on his coat, I could see that he was preoccupied, he was in the middle of writing a lengthy essay on Czech Cubism for the catalogue of a forthcoming exhibition. I looked at him fondly and reached out to touch his face. He was startled out of his thoughts and took my hand in his and held it as we made our way down the stairs and out into the cold air. I remember being perfectly happy, I remember wanting nothing more. The theater was only a short walk away from the apartment and I wished it were much further, miles further, so that we could continue to walk together in this way, and never arrive.

But we were soon a block away from the theater. Tomas stopped and said, I'm going to leave you now. And I saw that something had unlocked in his mind, that he was now ready to go to his desk, and that the silent walk through the cold air had done him good. Will you come with me as far as the café? I asked and he shook his head, he liked to have his coffee at home, at his elbow as he worked, I knew this already. I would rather go back, he said. I nodded and kissed him goodbye, a little reluctantly, and crossed the street alone.

A cyclist passed directly in front of me, I took a step back and then continued and perhaps because I was thus discombobulated I did not see Xavier until I had nearly reached the opposite side of the street. He was standing on the corner with his hands thrust into the pockets of his coat and his breath frosting the air. He was staring directly at me, from his posture I wondered if he had been standing there for some time, if he had observed the kiss I had given Tomas, the near collision with the cyclist.

I turned to see where Tomas had gone. The light had changed, I had crossed as it had flickered red and now the road was taken up with traffic, a slow-moving bus and then a taxi and a truck. Through the line of vehicles I saw Tomas on the opposite side of the street, still on the same corner, he hadn't moved. Xavier was now craning his neck to see what I was looking at and as I stepped forward he nodded and said, almost before I was within earshot, Is that your husband? And he stared at me with his large eyes, his expression placid.

How did you know that?

Know what?

That—

I turned to look back. Tomas was gone. I pulled open the door to the café and waved Xavier in, pulling the door closed behind me. Xavier was watching me thoughtfully.

I didn't know, he said after a moment.

Know what?

That he was your husband. I only asked. But it was a fair guess. You seemed very happy as you were walking beside him. Wasn't he at the restaurant? The other day?

I looked at him sharply.

Why do you ask?

No reason.

Were you waiting here for me?

No. It was a coincidence.

At that moment, the door opened and two women entered and we moved forward, to the side, to let them in. Gently, Xavier placed his hand on my back as he guided me away from the door and into the line. He cleared his throat and then spoke again.

I wanted to tell you that Anne has offered me a job.

I felt a flicker of dismay and shook my head.

How—

I was going to tell you at lunch but you left before I

could, and you were distracted, do you remember? He leaned forward, as if in order to make himself helpful, as if in order to help me recall.

I remember.

He paused, we had reached the front of the line. He indicated the woman standing behind the counter. What would you like?

I looked at the woman. An Americano. Xavier held up three fingers and the woman nodded and began to ring up the order. Before I could move, he had already pressed forward and paid against my protests. I'm getting one for Anne. Plus her breakfast sandwich. He smiled wryly. The production will cover it, he said and I nodded and went to the other side of the counter. He followed me and we stood together in silence until I spoke.

Why did Anne offer you a job? Did you ask for one?

No. I emailed her, as you know, and when she wrote back she said she was looking for a new assistant and asked if I was interested. This I knew was true, Lou had recently given notice, although I did not know the precise details and was not especially interested, Anne had a reputation for being difficult, but this was largely due to behavior that would pass unnoted in a male director. I asked to have lunch with you, Xavier persisted, because I wanted to tell you in advance, and because I wanted to clear the air after what I said that day when we first met, I wanted to make sure you were okay with it.

The woman placed our order on the counter and with a smooth movement Xavier picked it all up and carried it over to where the sugar and milks and lids were arrayed. To my astonishment, I found that the tables had in some way been turned, the entire time Xavier had only wanted to meet in order to inform me of his new position, to ensure there wouldn't be any awkwardness or bad feeling, suddenly I was the one who had imagined too much. Black? he asked over his shoulder, to my irritation, because he was correct and I did not like that he was correct. He pressed the lids onto the cups and then handed one to me and said, Shall we walk together?

His voice was mild and I had the feeling that had I told him I wanted to be alone, or that I wanted to sit in the café for a moment to gather my thoughts in advance of rehearsal, he would have acquiesced, and perhaps for that reason I perversely said yes. But he only smiled, his manner accommodating. There was no trace of the young man I had encountered only one week earlier, vibrating with uncertainty, he seemed to be a completely different person. As he held the door open for me, I saw that he was absorbed in, or had been absorbed by, the role of the assistant, that he was performing a part he had studied carefully, just as he had presumably studied the part of my long-estranged son. Like an actor moving on in the wake of a disastrous audition, shedding the skin of a role for which he had not been destined, and seeking out the next opportunity.

We stepped outside, I looked down the street but of course Tomas was gone. I took out my phone and sent him a message, wishing him a good day. And then I could delay no longer, and Xavier and I began walking down the street in the direction of the theater, coffees in hand, a little distance apart. For a brief moment, it seemed so natural that I felt embarrassed, that I had accused him of ambushing me on a street corner, that I had made this outlandish declaration.

But I was only working with what I knew, and it was no more outlandish—or rather, it was substantially less outlandish—than what he had said to me that day at the theater, and I reminded myself of his words, I recalled the scene in the theater café and then at the restaurant. The recollection came with force, but also some unreality, and I found myself wondering if I had misunderstood or misinterpreted or even misremembered the entire unlikely thing. It didn't seem possible to reconcile the scene now taking place, the two of us walking together in relative harmony, with the discordance of the scenes at the café and restaurant. He had succeeded in making the extraordinary tension between us grow diffuse, through the very naturalness of his manner, and I thought that if in those previous instances he had failed to impose his desired reality upon me, he had, at least this time, succeeded all too well.

The journalist misunderstood, I now said to Xavier. Some part of me would not let it lie, I wanted to return to the aperture, I wanted to force him to look at it again. Or rather she misrepresented the situation, I said. I have never had a child, I don't have children. You see, when I said it was impossible, I meant that quite literally.

I understand, he said. He sounded thoroughly rational, not at all like the kind of person who could have believed so fervently in a fantasy, let alone acted on it. He also seemed indifferent to my words, he stared straight ahead as we walked, although the pressure of my gaze was heavy on him. I saw a flicker of what I thought was consternation, and realized he was embarrassed on my behalf. After a pause, he asked, his voice almost excessively polite, You didn't want to have any?

And although the question was bold and even invasive, I replied. I don't know if I wanted to or not, at the time I thought I knew what I did and didn't want, but as you get older things become less clear. It wasn't anything that we had discussed at length between us, I continued. I mean me and Tomas, it was not a decision so much as something that simply happened. I fell silent. People always talked about having children as an event, as a thing that took place, they forgot that not having children was also something that took place, that is to say it wasn't a question of absence, a question of lack, it had its own presence in the world, it was its own event.

I looked at Xavier and gave a short laugh. I suppose by the time I thought about it with any degree of seriousness, I said, it was too late, and I was too old.

And your husband?

I didn't reply. It wasn't his business, what Tomas did or did not hope for. But the truth was I knew the exact shape of Tomas's desires, because of something that I had never discussed with anyone, something about which I for a long time felt—if not exactly troubled, then unresolved. What happened is this, I became pregnant a second time, and I did not immediately decide to have an abortion, but instead miscarried, eleven weeks into the pregnancy. This was far enough along so that the event was visceral and unmistakable, and I was in pain afterward, and there was not one but two trips to the hospital.

But—although that was not nothing, the physical process of passing the fetus or the embryo or the tissue, the range of possible words itself an indication of how mutable, how fraught the experience was, not something that could be swept under the carpet, it was among the more difficult experiences of my life, and I still did not know what to think about the fact that I had briefly borne death in my body— what actually stayed with me many years after the miscarriage itself was the texture of those two months, the two months between the positive test and the miscarriage, when I did not decide to have the baby but I did not decide to have an abortion either, and when the story of our life as a couple was suddenly open.

And while you might imagine—and sometimes even I could misremember the truth of how those eight or nine weeks passed—that it was a period of renewal, or hope, or whatever other words you might associate with the springtime of reproduction, even accidental and unintended reproduction, in fact it was something rather different, a remarkably cagey period between the two of us, when neither of us was entirely straightforward, entirely honest, about our feelings and desires, either with each other or with ourselves.

Eight or nine weeks. A period long enough for a different reality to assert itself, but not long enough for the seams stitching your old life together to come fully undone. Despite my ambivalence, I could feel my imagination work to take in this new idea, I could feel it twisting and ferreting out new positions, contorting into poses previously unimagined, until it could just about contain the thought. The thought of a baby in the world, a baby that belonged— although that was not the right word, its possessive nature describing the kind of relationship I did not wish to have, could not imagine having with another person—a baby that had to do with me, then. I could sometimes see, from the edges of my peripheral vision, a version of the world that was different from the one I occupied in this one critical factor, and therefore almost unrecognizable.

Tomas, on the other hand. It was different for Tomas, who had no difficulty imagining such a world, who'd had plenty of solitary practice. Tomas, for whom that world was always a blink away, so that if he simply squinted, it would come into focus. And for Tomas, in those two months, it was as if that world was within grasp. He was aware of my ambivalence, and so he was careful to hide the euphoria that now accompanied him everywhere, inconvenient and ir-repressible. I did not realize until then how much he had hoped for a child, and even now it pains me to remember how careful he was to conceal this from me, out of consid-eration but also out of a sense of shame at the extremity of his desire.

Still, it was only two weeks after the positive test that he secretly downloaded the app onto his phone, the one that would tell him what size the embryo was, vis-à-vis various species of fruit—blueberry, kumquat, eventually pineapple, although we never reached the pineapple stage, not even the lemon stage, the project folded at fig. But up until that point, probably up until that very day, he tracked the development of the embryo on the app, lost in private wonder at what was daily augmenting inside of me, this cluster of cells reproducing, the contemplation of which created a sense of awe that he did not feel able to share with me. He also did not share with me the calculations he made alone, late at night, about the odds of miscarriage, which grew longer with each passing day, a progress he followed doggedly and again, I emphasize, in private, until he began to think that perhaps we were in the clear, that his hope might not be disappointed, the tight cord of his anxiety broken, or at least a little slackened.

Of this, he never really spoke in detail, and once I had miscarried there was no way to talk about it that would not make our relationship even more brittle. But the app, with its strange and unappealing illustrations, I discovered earlier, while I was still pregnant. I picked up his phone from the counter and saw the open app, with its pastel images and exclamations. I put the phone down at once. It was the most bracing breach of his privacy I had ever performed, although it was unintentional, although I had done things in the past that were technically more invasive, I had eavesdropped on conversations, I had read his messages more than once, but none of those acts had felt transgressive in the same way, perhaps because I had discovered nothing surprising in those little incursions, nothing that altered my sense of our relationship, my sense of Tomas, so that I returned to myself, a little ashamed, but mostly reassured.

However, this was immediately something different, it was like coming upon my husband dressed in another person's clothes, I couldn't reconcile the essential austerity of Tomas's nature, the aesthetic precision of his taste, with the bouncing pea pods and cherries that danced across the screen, I believe there were even sparkles and confetti. It was a ridiculous way to think about a pregnancy. I recalled the way he had been, in those brief weeks, more than usually attached to his phone, there had been an almost tender intensity to the way he had consulted the device, so different from the usual irritation and worry with which he would scroll through the news or his messages. I realized that he had fallen into the cotton-candy world of the app, the soft corners of its feeling, he was using the app not despite its aesthetic but because of it.

In the end, it didn't matter, because I felt pain and then I was bleeding, and when I talked to other women they would say they knew or they intuited that something wasn't right, that you miscarry because something is wrong with the baby, but I didn't know and I didn't intuit anything, because this was the only time in my entire life that I would be pregnant in this way, for this long, that my body would carry another body. It was only a couple of months, not even twelve weeks, less if you count the days that I knew, still less if you only count the days after the pregnancy was confirmed. Although what did that confirmation mean in the end? It meant nothing, it was a mystery to me how something so fleeting could be considered confirmed, when its meaning could dissolve, without warning, into absence. But absence was not the right word, it penetrated further than that, because we did not speak of it to anyone else, because it remained, for all those years, a strictly private matter.

It was in the aftermath of the miscarriage that the affairs began in earnest. They were usually brief, they never threatened to encroach upon our marriage, although at times they could take me by surprise, I could become more absorbed than I intended. They were an expression of restlessness rather than discontent, of that I was certain. Still, it became increasingly difficult to find my way back to Tomas, and I was aware that the situation was becoming fraught, the apparatus of our marriage growing rickety, things could not continue in this way. I assumed Tomas knew about the affairs, perhaps some part of me was waiting for him to say something, to intervene, perhaps some part of me needed him to.

But he never said anything. He only waited. I never understood how he was so patient, so confident in my capacity to eventually see sense. In the days that followed each meaningless episode, all of which fizzled out unceremoniously, as they were bound to, after I returned to him shamefaced, as I was also always bound to, he never said anything to make me feel that there was a debt that needed repaying. He never even acknowledged the fact of betrayal. But there was a debt, of course there was, and I began to do small things in an attempt to address the yawning imbalance in our accounts.

Absurd as it sounds, among those things was the breakfast. It occurred to me one morning, when I woke early—the sign, you might say, of a guilty conscience, since I was never in those days an early riser—that I might set out breakfast for the two of us. Of course, because it was me, a person of relatively limited resources in this regard, all this meant was that I went down to the café and returned with some breakfast pastries, enough so that it could be called a selection. But when Tomas came into the kitchen to find me setting the pastries on a plate and pouring coffee, when I saw the expression of surprise on his face, an expression that he could not conceal—his astonishment had the force of a slap in the face, it startled me awake, and I was made to understand that it had been a long time since I had performed even so small an act of kindness.

He sat down. I sat down. We had breakfast. As we were clearing the plates and emptying the cups of coffee into the sink, Tomas put his hand on my arm, his fingers tightening so that I stopped what I was doing and turned to him in surprise. Then he suggested that we do it again, that we do it daily. He spoke with some insistence, so that I understood the question had meaning, as would my answer. I agreed, even though in that moment I didn't think I wanted to, not in the face of his demand, not in the face of my own inclination. I assumed it wouldn't actually happen. But it did, first for a week, and then for a month, and then for so long that it became habit and routine, and in that small act of domesticity, I recommitted myself to the marriage. It was banal, indisputably bourgeois, the coffee cups and the stupid pastries—but that was almost the point. To return to that ordinary life, with its coziness and safety, all those things that are so easy to despise and dismiss. In those rituals of daily life, I committed myself to the marriage, in all its mundanity, all over again. At least for a time.

5

Of course, I did not say any of this to Xavier. Instead, we walked in a silence that he seemed in no rush to break. I saw an elderly couple take note of us as we passed, this time it was clear that what they saw in us was not some unsavory sexual entanglement but rather the contrary, a wholesome outing between a mother and son. They wore expressions of approval and general goodwill, as if we were manifesting a socially constructive relationship, as opposed to the socially destructive one the couple at the restaurant believed themselves to have seen. I thought it must have been because of the apparent ease between us, we must have seemed like two people between whom there is nothing that is particularly troublesome, nothing hanging heavy in the air. We had passed the couple when Xavier said, I'm glad that we were able to speak, I would have hated for you to have just walked into the theater and found me there. I guess it would have been an unpleasant surprise.

I laughed despite myself. Somewhat, I said, and it was true, I had a sudden vision of how I would have felt, entering the darkened theater, had I seen Xavier and Anne, sitting close together, bent over their notes, the slow raising of Xavier's head, Anne's hand as she waved me over. But as I looked at the young man beside me—so young he could still safely be called a boy—the idea seemed very far away, as if it came from the dream of another person.

You can be entranced by an idea, I said, and at a certain point you can no longer see the edges of it. Xavier watched me attentively, as if the words in some way followed what had just been said. But of course they did, they were a kind of peace offering or confession. I've experienced it myself, I continued, it's something that happens every time I prepare for a role. In some ways the part is only working if I lose sight of the shore. But at the same time, it's important to be able to come out the other side, you have to be able to come up for air. Otherwise, you won't survive.

He nodded and I fell silent. This had not always been an issue, for a long time there had been a gap between the fullness of the life I felt inside me, which like all lives was complex and contradictory, experience stratifying into the matter that makes up a person—there had been a gap between this internal landscape and the near comical flatness of the parts I was given to play, made up as they were of clichés and stereotypes, empty of imagination.

For people like me, who looked like me, there were no parts—or rather, there were only parts that were commensurate with erasure, whether through the thinness of stereotype or through simple marginalization, often these characters were quite literally silent, a moving image and nothing else. I suppose it was even worse because I was a woman. At one point, my agent had suggested that I might change my name, he said that there was something racially indeterminate about my appearance, with a different name there would be better parts. Parts—a word that implied that there were parts and then there was a whole, into which those parts might cohere, a whole that might be a play or a film or a series, a whole that might even be a career, a body of work that could exist in the public imagination.

Of course, I was not indeterminate to myself, and I did not change my name. And for a long time, it did not seem likely that my work would achieve that totality, whether I changed my name or not. I had time to wonder what it meant, who the work was made and performed for, whose

imagination I was being subjugated to, because I knew it was
not my own. As a consequence, for many years I did my work
without fully committing myself to it. Even as the parts improved, I never confused the experience depicted onstage or
on-screen with the experience of my actual life, the material simply did not have the requisite dimensionality, there
was nothing in these parts that had the stab, the throb, the
unruliness of the real.

But things changed. The film with Murata was important, even in a language I was speaking more or less phonetically, I was more a person in that role than I had ever been
before. People saw me differently after that, and the success
of the film happened to coincide with a change in the culture, in the writing, a change in the way of seeing. For the
first time, I was allowed to be human. I could even be at the
center of a story. And later still, there were parts that con-
sumed me, so that I could say the life that was performed,
on a set or in the theater, could at times feel more real to me
than my actual life. This change in the culture represented
a tremendous gift, without it all the parts that followed,
including this one with Anne, they would not have been
possible. But it was also a danger for a person of my disposition, for whom the managing of these borders was not always easy.

Xavier asked if I had been able to immerse myself in my

new part, if that process had taken place, and I looked up at him, startled out of my thoughts. He was gazing at me with a placid expression, not in the least as if he were asking a sensitive question. And yet he had touched upon something that was in fact a vulnerability, he had found with unerring intuition something that was now beginning to trouble me. I wondered how innocent the question was, if Anne had said something to him, if she could also tell that things were not progressing as they should. Perhaps that was even the reason why he had been waiting at the corner, outside the café where I always picked up a coffee on my way in to rehearsal, perhaps all this time it was Anne who had sent him.

It would have been fair for her to be concerned, we were three weeks into rehearsal, and I'd had an unusually long time to prepare, and yet I still felt myself too much to be playing a part, I couldn't seem to locate the center of the role. This wasn't necessarily unusual, in the past there had been plenty of parts that had continued to elude me, even as the work as a whole improved—whether through my own failing or a failing in the writing or the direction or something else altogether. The alchemy was particular, and the truth was that there were many occasions when it went awry, or did not cohere, I had come to see it as something of a crapshoot, you never knew if this would be the one when everything would come together or if it would fall by the wayside, another disposable performance, the detritus of a soon to be forgotten artistic endeavor.

But in the case of this part, this production, I had every reason to hope for the best, not only was I working with Anne, but the play had been written by a playwright I had long admired. She was a young writer, exceptionally brilliant, I had seen an early production of hers at a small theater downtown that seated no more than eighty people. The theater was half empty the night I went (although that changed as soon as the reviews came in, breathless and ecstatic, then the tickets sold out for weeks in advance and the run was extended twice, three times, by which point the writer had been garlanded in awards and commissions and offered a place in several writers' rooms) but even in a half-empty theater with a cast of unknowns, I knew that she was an extraordinary talent. Tension grew out of every scene, scenes in which nothing took place and people said very little, and yet the pressure grew and grew so that by the end of the play I realized I had been in a sickening state of unease for some time, and when I emerged from the theater I was simultaneously invigorated and physically exhausted, every nerve in my body still standing on end.

Of course, I immediately called my agent and asked her to arrange a meeting, and not too long after that I spoke to

Anne, who had also seen the young playwright's work and been similarly impressed. However, everyone had been by then, so it was by no means assured that we would have the opportunity to work with her, much less that she would make a new piece with us. But as it turned out, after nearly two years of expressions of intent and little more, she suddenly called me and said she had something. When she sent me the play I knew from the first page that this was the part for me, the one that came along only very rarely, and that if I was patient and careful it could form the basis of the best work I had ever done.

But then, after the first table read, and after the early rehearsals and the later rehearsals, and even as Anne and the playwright herself extolled the virtues of my interpretation, even as the pieces began to fall into place and the shape of the performances began to emerge—my own, and also those of the rest of the cast—and even as I began to see in the not too distant future the point at which the emergence would cease and the structure of the work begin to ossify, so that although some movement would remain possible, its essential parameters would be set—even then, I had the sense that I was still too much clinging to the shore. The part, the world of it, continued to elude me, and I knew that the window of opportunity was closing, that I had to make some shift within myself or the role would slip away.

I had been silent for some time, and now I said, There is only one more week of rehearsal, and then we go into tech.

Anne said that you are already excellent.

I am not where I need to be. I'm waiting for something to happen and time is running out. I moved my head uneasily, I didn't know why I was telling Xavier this. There is always the chance that the breakthrough takes place later, I said. But I'm starting to fear I won't get there. He nodded sympathetically, as if he understood what I was saying, although that seemed unlikely, I hardly knew what I was saying myself. It's not through any fault of Anne's, I added. The play itself is wonderful. It's me.

But what if you are actually good? Does it matter how you feel?

Of course it matters, I said quickly. But even as I spoke I found myself uncertain. Did it matter? It mattered in the sense that the work was what counted—not the activity that surrounded it, the energy that collected or dissipated upon its reception. But I didn't know how to separate the work from its effect. I recalled a recent film centered on a performance that had seemed to me so extraordinary it had recast everything I knew about the actor, whom I had previously found rather uninteresting despite his storied career and reputation, as he had gotten older there was a palpable laziness to his work, the sense that he could no longer be bothered to rouse himself to his former heights, he was always playing some previous version of himself, the version that had won the acclaim and sealed the reputation.

But in this film, in *Salvation*, he had produced a performance of rare depth and complexity, recalling the promise he showed at the very start of his career, when he still seemed moved by ambition and curiosity. He played each scene with painful caution, reaching out to touch a table, a counter, as if seeking to be grounded, I could feel the character's turmoil in almost every instant on-screen. He would look down and then up again and there would be an expression of such confusion on his face that it was not too much to say that my heart broke as I watched him. I had to admit that I'd been wrong about him, he was in fact an actor of remarkable subtlety and commitment, and I subsequently agreed to work with him.

But soon after we arrived on set, to my surprise I found that he was as vacuous and vain as I had previously thought, and as we began to rehearse I felt a jolt of distress, he seemed to have little sense of the scene and he knew none of his lines, he kept dipping his head down into the script and mouthing the words to himself, for all the world as if he had never so much as seen them in his life. I felt frustration and even anger, it was hard not to take it as a sign of disrespect, after all he was wasting my time and the time of everyone on set, he was even wasting his own time, of which, I remember thinking maliciously, he did not have a great deal remaining.

Perhaps sensing my exasperation, the director pulled me aside and said that the actor was having trouble memorizing his lines and was unlikely to recall any of them, and that I should be prepared for this, I shouldn't expect matters to improve. I looked at him in confusion, and he explained that he had spoken to Stan, the director of *Salvation*. I should have told you earlier, he said, but the truth is I only just found out. He can't remember his lines. He turned up on the set of *Salvation* every day without knowing any of his lines.

I gave a short laugh of disbelief and the director raised his hand, as if to stop me. At first Stan thought it was simply lack of focus and preparation, but quite soon he realized that it was beyond his control, he really couldn't retain the words for even the minute between looking at the script and delivering them from inside the scene. So they stuck notes with the lines on every surface of the set and muddled through. Do you remember the scene in the kitchen, when he's running his hands across the counter? That's him looking for his note. Same in the bathroom scene.

I stared at the director is disbelief. As it turned out, he continued wryly, the result was genuinely remarkable, and it was on that basis that I cast him in this movie, the one we are now making, or trying to, at least. It was only later that I discovered the source of the performance's strength, which is the fact that it is no performance at all. That confusion that you see on-screen is completely real. You are looking at a man lost, with no sense of what the story is, trapped inside the scene, with the camera lens staring at him, you are watching a man who is seeing his life and his career drift away.

But why didn't Stan tell you? I asked. It works for that movie, I admit—and here I stopped and nodded to myself. I admit it works very well for that, I said. But for this—

I know, the director said. When Stan told me, I was furious. Why didn't you warn me? I asked him. Stan simply said that he would have felt as if he were betraying the actor. For such a story to become public—for such a story even to circulate within the industry would be fatal. It wasn't that he felt especially loyal to the actor, he was more than happy to complain about his vanity and his bullheadedness, it was in this one regard that he felt a kind of fidelity. He had even attempted to hide the degree of the actor's impairment from the crew, he had not said that the actor was suffering from dementia, but instead claimed that he had refused to learn his lines, that he was lazy, stupid, words of abuse that were in fact designed to protect the actor, to prevent the others from guessing the terrible truth.

You see, the director said, in his way Stan loved him. Yes, I said, or perhaps it was the performance he loved, and the process of extracting it. On some level, what Stan had done was ruthless and unconscionable, he must have known that he had crossed a moral line, and I couldn't help but feel that it was the secret of that transgression—not the aging actor, not even the reputation of the film—that Stan was so eager to protect.

In any case, our film had not replicated the success of *Salvation*, although the actor continued to muddle through and work came to him as frequently as before, probably even now he was somewhere on set, wandering through a scene. At the time, I remember being shocked and also disillusioned by the disclosure, it changed the way I saw the performance. After my conversation with the director I went back and re-watched the film and all I could see was a man with incipient dementia, lost on-screen, searching restlessly for his lines, for the words he knew he was meant to be saying. But now, as Xavier walked alongside me, it occurred to me that the performance did remain—that is to say, the performance I had experienced the first and even second time I watched the film remained extant, and I thought that it was true that a performance existed in the space between the work and the audience, that it existed, and was made, in that space of interpretation.

But then I also thought that if ever an actor had lost sight of the shore then it was this one, he had stumbled deep into the interior, and I wondered if he worried that he would never find his way out, if the world of fiction had lost its protective powers, the line between reality and invention undone. The confusion and the vulnerability that I had seen on-screen was real enough. And I thought again of the panic in the actor's eyes, which was entirely authentic, when he stood in the middle of the set, when he looked at the other actors, the director, for his scrap of paper, in that moment everything was terribly, terrifyingly real.

Because of course, there was another element to the performance in *Salvation*, which was death. And although the actor was only in his sixties, as soon as I heard the story of the notes on the counter, the forgotten lines—not even forgotten, because they had not been retained and then lost again, they had evaded his mind's grasp altogether—as soon as I heard this, I was able to envision his death. I was able to imagine the parabolic arc of his decline, I understood that eventually his mind would disintegrate to the point that his memory, of the world and of himself, would be lost, and with it everything that formed his being. It was death, that was what we had responded to when we watched him wading through those scenes on-screen, even if we hadn't understood it. The film was a portrait of a man in the process of surrender.

I no longer knew how I felt about *Salvation*, a work I had

previously enjoyed in such a pure and naïve way, that innocence was gone. I understood all too well what I was seeing. And I wondered also if that wasn't the point of a performance, that it preserved our innocence, that it allowed us to live with the hypocrisies of our desire. Because in fact we don't want to see the thing itself, on a screen or on a stage, we don't want to see actual pain or suffering or death, but its representation. Our awareness of the performance is what allows us to enjoy the emotion, to creep close to it and breathe in its atmosphere, performance allows this dangerous proximity.

Without it, *Salvation* was only a snuff film. And so I said to Xavier that it did matter, yes, it did. Without intentionality, there was no agency, no control, the work was happening to you. An impossible inversion.

Ah, he said lightly, and he took a sip of coffee. We had arrived at our destination.

6

WE STOOD OUTSIDE THE THEATER DOORS. XAVIER HELD the two coffees aloft, one in each hand, the bag with the breakfast sandwich. He carried the second cup with care, his fingers delicately braced around its edge, and somehow in his pose and in that little paper cup I could see the entire dynamic of his relationship with Anne. I didn't need to see the two together in order to understand how they would interact, and then I recalled, although I didn't know how I could have forgotten, that he would be present throughout the remainder of the rehearsal period and beyond. He smiled, a mild smile without insinuation.

I'm not sure you're right.

What?

I think your performance is probably pretty good, even if you don't feel that way.

I laughed, a sudden, indecorous sound. Well, I hope for my sake that's true.

I opened the door to the building and waved him in, still smiling, coffees in hand. We crossed the empty lobby and I opened the door to the theater too, so that he entered first and I saw again how the attention in the room moved toward him at once. I was not exactly envious, which is too general a word, encompassing too large a range of feeling. But the moment was a reminder of the invisibility that was rapidly approaching, increasingly I could walk down the street or pass through a room without occasioning notice, in a way that I remembered longing for when I was younger, when I was Xavier's age.

Of course, here I was not actually invisible, in this particular room I had a kind of status and through this a visibility, even if it was dependent on context. Anne looked up and hurried toward us, before suddenly stopping and clapping her hands together in an expression of surprise or delight.

Don't you make the perfect mother and son, she said with a laugh.

Almost, Xavier answered.

I didn't say anything, and a shadow of irritation crossed Anne's face, directed not at me or Xavier but at herself, probably she thought that I would take umbrage at a comment that seemed designed to remind me of my age. Or perhaps she worried that her words had betrayed a racial assumption, revealed that to her, we all looked the same. She stretched out a hand for her coffee and Xavier gave it to her, along with the paper bag containing her breakfast sandwich. He had a surprising air of competence, completely at odds with the personality he had exhibited before, again I thought he was like another person entirely. I saw that he had a soothing effect on Anne, his movements had a muted calm and efficiency, like a trainer expert at handling skittish animals.

As I watched him moving quietly but attentively around her, as I observed the easy intimacy that had already been established between them, I understood why Anne had said that we could be mother and son. It was not because of the physical similarity between me and Xavier, or it was not only or even mainly because of that. It was because Anne had recognized in Xavier an archetypal son. He fell into the role, performing filial affection and duty, creating an atmosphere that Anne had been compelled to name, if only unconsciously and indirectly. She had not, I realized, been speaking of me but of herself, and that glint of frustration, that had not been because she worried that she might have insulted me—I should have known better, after all she knew me too well for that—but because consciously or unconsciously she worried that she had in some way revealed herself.

Xavier gave good son. He loved the part of it, he longed for the role, that was why he had contacted me in the first place. He was now giving good son to Anne, and she was responding, and through that mutuality a membrane had formed around them. I moved down the aisle, away from them, and stared at the empty stage. I took a sip of coffee. Xavier seemed to feel toward me no differently than he felt toward Anne, or rather he seemed to feel toward me somewhat less than what he felt toward Anne. My gaze slipped back to them, they were standing with their heads close together, Anne was speaking animatedly, Xavier said something in response and Anne laughed, looking up at him affectionately. For a moment I felt a throb of envy, the sense that I had given up something without being wholly aware of what it was.

Anne came over and sat down in the front row and began eating the sandwich Xavier had brought her. She motioned to the seat beside her and I sat down. Chewing vigorously, she wiped her mouth with a napkin and nodded to me.

How do you feel about how things are going?

Fine, I said immediately.

It's coming along faster than I expected. Every day there are discoveries that push the thing forward. I can feel—she lifted her hands and clenched them, the sandwich resting in her lap—I can feel it coming. And Max is happy. Anne paused and turned to look at me. You know, before we started I spoke to Max and she warned me that she was exacting. You can make it your own, she said. It doesn't need to be true to my vision. But it needs to be true.

Anne pried the lid off her coffee and took a sip before she continued. That's not the kind of message I generally find helpful, and I told her so outright. How was I supposed to know if it was true? By whose standards? What does such a word even mean? But then, as we started working with the material, I began to understand, there's an integrity to each scene that emerges over time. At one point during rehearsal last week, I looked over at Max and she looked back at me and she nodded and although the scene was not the scene I had read on the page, although the scene was possibly not even what she had actually written, I knew that Max approved. Later, she told me that she was happy.

What exactly did she say?

Just that she was happy. That things were going well. We still have a week before tech. There are elements to be worked out but she feels confident we'll get there.

Anne took another bite of her sandwich.

The things to be worked out—

She searched for her napkin and I handed it to her impatiently. She wiped her mouth again.

Yes, well, the scene we're working on today is one of them.

I had expected her to say as much. Over the course of the past three weeks, scene after scene had come together, in the way that Anne described. Max was not alone, that nervous exhilaration had been shared by the entire cast, at one point Clarice had pulled me aside and told me that the play was not about what she had thought it was about, that it was better, subtle and more mysterious. I had watched the work emerge with incredible rapidity, until it was only one particular scene, positioned right in the middle of the play, that remained patently unresolved. It sat in the center like a black hole or box, and it was a scene that I played alone. This was the material that we were going to work on today.

I stared at the empty and unlit stage. Of the cast, I had been the first to grasp the mercurial brilliance of Max's work, the slippery and insidious way the scenes emerged, it was only when you dwelled inside the material that the essence of the drama grew apparent. But the scene we were working on today, the one that Max was unhappy with— because although Anne did not say so directly, it was obvious that this was what she meant—that scene continued to resist me, it was the one thing I couldn't fully parse, and without it I was unable to make sense of the part as a whole. I had been aware of this problem within the play for some time, and of late I had begun to wonder if in fact there was some hollowness in the construction of the scene itself. The structure and the narrative of the play demanded that the scene contain a process of transformation, a moment of alchemy and transition, but in truth I couldn't find the basis for that metamorphosis in what had been written on the page.

I got to my feet.

Is Max here?

Anne nodded, tilting her head back very slightly. I turned and saw Max standing at the rear of the theater, she appeared to be on the phone. She looked over and waved at me before turning away. I crossed the theater, as she saw me approaching she spoke rapidly into her phone and then hung up. She gave me a quick but somehow wary hug, as if she knew what I was going to say, or as if she would soon be telling me or telling Anne there was a problem. She took a step back, still gripping her phone in her hand, putting a little more distance between us, and then asked how I was feeling, in almost the exact tone that Anne had used, so that I began to suspect they had already spoken and determined that the problem was, in fact, me.

I'm fine.

Good. I talked to Anne. We want to nail down this scene today. There's still something a little indeterminate about it. But can I be honest? I simultaneously nodded and shook my head, I didn't know if I wanted her to be honest. This scene is different from anything else in the play, it's different from anything else I've written. She frowned. It's more schematic, or rather it's only schematic. Everything I write is based in excavating the minutiae of emotion, inhabiting the nooks and crannies of an encounter. But this is more conceptual. It's arid, cold. She nodded to me. Much like your character.

As she spoke, I was a little taken by surprise, I had not especially thought of the character as cold. She made a little grimace, as if she had a bad or bitter taste in her mouth, she seemed to feel a certain amount of contempt toward the very character she had created and centered her story around, a woman racked by grief, by the extinction of possibility, a shell of a person no longer able to fully access her own emotions. That was how I understood the character, but I saw in the flicker of her eyes that even if I was correct, even if this was the character as she had conceived of it, she not only held her and her grief in some disdain, she was also—and this was perhaps worse—a little bored by her. I felt at once defensive of the character, and also of myself, if she was so bored by her character, then it followed that she was also bored by my performance.

She carried on, oblivious or indifferent to my consternation, which I was unable to hide. Of course, this is the moment when your character achieves a kind of breakthrough, and reaches the opposite shore. *The Opposite Shore* was the title of the play, but she said it without any irony or self-consciousness, perhaps she always found her own writing eminently quotable. It's absolutely central, she continued. It is the moment when she locates her emotion, when the play breaks opens, when she steps forward into life, if you see.

She shook her fist, the one holding the phone, it was almost a little fist pump, and then she nodded as if she had clarified matters in some useful way, as if I had now been given the key to unlock this black box of a scene, but the truth was I had almost no idea what she was talking about, it was all a way of talking rather than talking itself. The sensation of dread increased. Max was looking at me but when I stared back her face closed down a little, as if she had been confronted, and I knew then that she had no idea what she had written, no idea of how it would work in the play, how it would bridge the two versions of the character, the scene she had written was nothing more than a placeholder. She had grown bored of the character in the midst of writing, I realized, and wanted to write a different character, and so had created this impossible scene to segue between not two versions of the same character, but two different characters altogether. I could see it now, I could see it all over the writing. She gazed back at me and I noted the fear in her eyes and then she held up her phone and said, I'm so sorry but I need to take this, and dove through the exit of the theater.

The phone hadn't even been ringing. I returned to my seat and exhaled, I would need to make sense of the part as she had written it, I understood that she had, essentially, no idea how to fix the rickety transition between the two halves of the play, the movement from the woman in grief to the woman of action. I snapped the script open. I was frustrated and uneasy, exactly the wrong state of mind for this work.

Xavier rose to his feet and came to me. Is everything okay? he asked. Do you need anything? I stared at the script, his eyes also went down to the page. He said, This is the scene you're doing today? I nodded. Any tips? I asked drily. He shrugged. My dad used to tell me a joke, although at the time it was a story rather than a joke. I nodded and waited for him to continue. He said that he had a friend who was no longer in love with his wife, no longer took joy in his children, but who nonetheless did not want to leave his family. He only wanted to feel the way he used to feel. He asked his therapist what to do. She told him to pretend he was in love with his wife. To enact it as fully as possible, and then eventually, he would be in love with her again.

Why is this a joke? I asked irritably and checked the time. Anne was getting to her feet, brushing the crumbs of her breakfast sandwich off her lap.

Oh, he said. Because he was talking about himself. My mom was the wife he was no longer in love with, and me and my brother and my sister were the children who no longer gave him joy. After he had done what his therapist told him to do and fallen in love with my mom again, we used to joke about it.

That's not funny, I said.

I know. But it felt funny at the time.

You have a mother?

He gave me a strange look. Anne came down the aisle in front of us. Have you seen Max?

She had to take a call, I said shortly.

Do you want me to— And Xavier rose to his feet.

Please, Anne said. We need to start.

She looked after him affectionately as he disappeared down the aisle. You know, she said, I think it could really work out with Xavier. It's a stroke of luck that he emailed me. Because of you, in fact—and here she turned to me, face expectant, but I merely nodded. It turns out he's a friend of Hana's, she said after a pause. Robbie and Mieko's daughter. They're in school together.

He seems very comfortable with you.

He anticipates. So many of my assistants have been reactive. It's nice to have someone who can anticipate my needs.

There was a softness to her expression, a vagueness, that somehow vexed me further, I saw that she had decided to take Xavier under her wing, that he would be a fixture now, present at all times, privy to Anne's thoughts about her work and beyond, her assistants were always required to absorb a great deal, both in terms of emotion and in terms of information. Many of them did not last, Anne had a great deal of energy and she was demanding, you had to give yourself over to her, something that was enticing when you were an actor or a collaborator of hers, someone for whom the vision was reason and seduction enough, but was perhaps less compelling to the young men and women who were obliged to fetch her coffees and run her errands.

However, I could already see that Xavier would succeed, not simply because he was exceptionally mutable but because that mutability did not seem to cost him very much. He did not seem any less himself, he did not seem to be troubled or even to feel those shifts in his being. I thought again about his gentle questioning as we walked to the theater, his manner had been completely natural, I could not believe that he had asked the questions at Anne's behest, and yet it also did not seem impossible that he and Anne had discussed the difficulties I was experiencing, not impossible to imagine that Anne and Xavier and even Max, that the three of them had discussed the matter together. I felt further irritation, it was unpleasant to imagine them combing over the weaknesses of my interpretation, which were in fact weaknesses in the writing. She hasn't seized the part at all, they might have said, she hasn't understood it.

I still hated the idea of people talking behind my back, and this was worse because I was now convinced that Max would have tried to put some of the responsibility—if not the blame, I still had respect for Max, although I was beginning to see her in a different light—onto me. It made me revert to the state of being a child, and it was in this state that I leaned forward and said to Anne, When we first met, Xavier told me something strange. Even as I said it, I was not proud, because I knew it was petty and because I knew I was reacting out of insecurity and pique, and also because despite everything, I felt that what Xavier had said was in some way a secret, something private that should not be shared, although of course I owed him nothing, nor had he asked me not to speak of what he had said and done.

Anne looked at me attentively, as if to ask what it was I

wanted to say, but not, I don't think, with any particular anxiety or concern, it was impossible for her to imagine that there could be anything untoward about the young man. At that moment, just as I was about to speak, my phone vibrated. It was a message from Tomas and I swiped to read it. We need to talk, he wrote. I am writing because I worry that if I do not write, if I do not commit to these words, I will lose my nerve and avoid the issue again. And yet it won't do to carry on in this way.

I put the phone down in my lap.

What is it? Anne asked.

I looked up. A message from Tomas.

No, she said. I mean about Xavier.

Nothing, I said. In that moment, I forgot about Max and the play and the scene, whatever paranoid ideas had been scurrying through my mind, the natural frustrations of re-hearsal, suddenly all proportion had been restored. I need to call Tomas, I said and Anne shook her head. Her eyes had gone up to the theater doors, and when I turned I saw that Max and Xavier had returned. I looked at Xavier, at his calm and placid face, the reassuring smile that he seemed to give to me, and to my surprise, I felt a starburst of longing. I was about to get to my feet when Anne snapped her head back to me. Not now, she said. And her voice was surprisingly firm. She made a gesture to Max and Xavier, motioning them to come down, and then she clambered up onto the stage, coffee in hand, the coffee that Xavier had brought for her. She set the cup on the floor and then straightened to her full height. Okay, she said, and she clapped her hands together, once. We've wasted enough time. We begin now.

PART II

7

We were seated at a table for three, in the center of the restaurant, beneath a spotlight. Our faces were in partial shadow, moving in and out of the light as we spoke, sat back, as we took up the menus and reached for our glasses. It was the same restaurant where I had met Xavier for lunch, all those months ago, before he began working with Anne, before the success of *Rivers*, although this time we were together, the three of us: me, Tomas, and Xavier.

Once we had ordered, Tomas reached for his wine and said he wanted to toast the extraordinary success of the play. As he lifted his glass I gazed at Tomas and then at Xavier, their faces soft and smiling in the light, united in the same expression, each an echo of the other. It was true that the success of the play had exceeded all expectation. *Rivers* had been extended three times and still the run was sold out, the tickets gone almost as soon as they were made available. The reviews had been uniform, they had been ecstatic, to the degree that we were even at times tempted to believe they might be true.

And while Max and Anne had received due recognition, the praise had largely fallen upon me and my performance. Never before had I received such universal approbation, never before had my work been scrutinized and interpreted so thoroughly, or indeed so warmly. It had sent my agents into a frenzy, every other day they seemed to contact me with offers, for film and television and theater, some of which were even interesting, and many of which I would have accepted with excitement only months earlier.

But I was, for the moment, living outside my ambition, still so ensnared in the world of Max's play that I could not imagine leaving. I recalled the frustration I had felt during the rehearsal period, the doubts I'd had about Max's writing—all that was now impossible to fathom, I couldn't understand what I had been feeling. She was without question the best writer I had ever worked with, the part and the play the best material I had ever been given to perform. In *Rivers*, she had created a role of seemingly endless depth and variation, so that no two performances were the same. Whereas a role tends to grow more solid and predictable over the course of a play's run, in the case of *Rivers* there was no such process of accumulation, the performance never seemed to settle, each time I walked onto the stage I did not know what would happen, which version of the part and the story would come to me. I felt I could play the role a thousand times and still not reach the end, the boundaries of its world, I felt there would always be more to explore.

And the scene that had troubled me so deeply, it had become the scene I looked forward to the most, the transition from the first half of the play into the second, the instant of transformation—the play's hinge. As soon as I arrived at the theater I could not wait to be inside the scene, I anticipated the music cue, the pool of light emerging on the near darkness of the stage. I longed for it in a way that was almost carnal. When I breathed in and stepped forward into the light, countless paths seemed to unfurl before me, forking and then forking again, so that I was dazzled each time by the scene's infinite contingency, the range of possibility laid out in front of me.

From that point, for a period of four minutes and thirty-odd seconds, I explored the scene's terrain. The experience felt wholly private, even though I was onstage. It was not that I forgot about the audience or the parameters and construction of the set. It was that here, the gap between my private and performed selves collapsed, and for the briefest of moments there was only a single, unified self. Did this happen only in those few minutes on that stage and nowhere else? It felt that way. Although every beat of the scene was tightly scripted, I felt as if I had an infinite amount of time, I moved at my leisure. And while I hit my marks and cues, never deviating from the script, I was not in control of what took place, there was an alchemical process by which the scene unfolded, mysterious even to me and Max. In those moments, I was in communion with something, some force that was larger than myself and the scope of my ordinary life.

It would not be too much to say that I was never certain who I would be when I emerged from that scene. And because of this, despite the fact that Anne and Max had since moved on to other projects—projects that had been booked in advance, and new projects as well, so that both their schedules were full for the next few years and they could take on nothing more—I'd always known that I would remain with *Rivers* through to the end of its run. Xavier had of course moved on with Anne, his role growing larger by the day, she now relied heavily upon him. It was not only in the daily administration of her life—although it was also that, he was surprisingly adept at resolving small crises, scheduling conflicts, flight delays, all those minutiae, a skill I never could have guessed or imagined he possessed—he was becoming more than an assistant, he was beginning to take a creative role, she had even floated the possibility that he might be assistant director on her current project. Privately, she told me that he had talent, that he had sensibility—a word she frequently used, but that really did apply to Xavier, who had nothing if not an excess of sensibility.

But really, I was delighted. Of course, I missed his regular presence at the theater, which had lightened the weight of those final days of rehearsal leading into previews, when it was not yet clear whether or not we had succeeded, not yet clear whether or not I would break open the part and inhabit it, I had to admit that his presence had grounded me. I had not expected it, I thought it would make me feel constrained and self-conscious, to perform in front of him. But Xavier was the perfect observer, at once present and neutral, when you stepped from the stage he didn't gush or deliver notes, unlike so many people he did not feel the need to fill in the performance with words and interpretation, he simply let it be.

In the last weeks of rehearsal, when both Anne and Max had been worried and preoccupied, I myself had relied on Xavier, something that recalibrated our relationship. For the first month or two after we opened, even after Anne had turned to her next project, he continued to come to the theater every evening, sometimes to pick me up and often to see the show, he told me that much in the way that I never seemed to tire of performing the role, so he never tired of watching the play and its endless mutations. After, we would walk together to the restaurant around the corner and meet Tomas for dinner. Sometimes Josie or Clarice would join us, or Anne if she happened to be in the neighborhood.

Whenever Anne joined, I was always aware of the delicate negotiation taking place between Xavier, Anne, and me—Anne, who was Xavier's mentor and employer, someone who had taken a meaningful interest in him, Anne, who was in the process of making introductions and opening doors, who was involving him in creative decisions and who listened closely when he spoke, this attention alone transformative, it allowed Xavier to see himself differently, to imagine new possibilities—Anne on the one hand, and me on the other, Xavier's mother.

I knew I had to give Xavier space, to be himself rather than my son, and it was also true that I had every reason to wish for the relationship between Anne and Xavier to flourish. In this sense, in giving him space I was also giving her space, which she was all too eager to claim. Still, it was not possible to occlude the reality of my relationship with Xavier, the affinities and understandings built over a lifetime. I could see that he was not entirely at ease with Anne, he was not unaware of the reasons she was drawn to him, he understood that what was being enacted between them was not simply a mentor and protégé relationship, but something else as well.

The other night, she had arrived at the restaurant a little late, so that we were already seated and had already ordered, although Xavier had been texting her throughout, sending her a photo of the menu, taking her order, and conveying it to the waiter, Tomas and I had observed him with some wonder, never had we imagined that he could be so attentive. I remember that I felt some small alarm, that he should be so altered, it must have shown on my face because Tomas reached out and gently squeezed my hand, as if to remind me that this was the change we had long hoped for, this was the change we wanted.

In any case, Xavier had conveyed Anne's order to the waiter, including all the necessary modifications, of which there were a fair number, and then we settled down to conversation, it had been over a week since I had last seen Xavier and I was eager to hear his news. He spoke quickly, there was a great deal that he wanted to share about his work with Anne, and I remember that we were deep in conversation when at last she appeared at the table. When I lifted my head, I saw that she wore an expression of consternation and I nearly asked if anything was wrong, if something had happened.

Xavier told her that he had placed her order, her timing was perfect and the food should be arriving soon. She didn't reply, she only looked irritably at Xavier, who sat between me and Josie, and then at her own seat between Tomas and Clarice, on the other side of what was quite a large table. I saw a rapid calculation take place in her mind before she edged her way around the table and tapped Josie on the shoulder. I'm afraid Xavier and I still have a few work things to discuss, she said. Do you mind swapping seats? Josie stared at her in amazement, and then slowly got to her feet.

Anne was in the chair almost before Josie had vacated it and promptly monopolized Xavier's attention. Tomas and I exchanged glances, across the table Josie appeared, if not exactly put out, then mildly annoyed, she kept interrupting their conversation in order to ask Anne to pass her water glass, her napkin and cutlery, the phone she had left on their side of the table. I was aware that I was the one that Anne really wished to displace, figuratively and possibly literally, she probably would have pushed me out of my seat had it not been difficult for reasons of age and position and because, I suppose, it would have seemed rather obvious. Still, at one point Xavier turned to ask me about some reference or another, to a novel I think it was, affectionately gripping my hand in his, and I saw Anne's eyes dart down to our hands and then back to Xavier's face, she seemed barely able to conceal her avidity.

Of course, in these situations, Anne ceded to me—she knew that her jealousy was unreasonable and even embarrassing, somehow worse than being jealous over a man for strictly sexual reasons, and certainly more revealing. I understood well enough that some part of Anne wished that she, rather than I, was Xavier's mother, even if she didn't articulate it in so many words, and even if she was aware that no relationship was without its difficulties, had she actually been Xavier's mother they could not have enjoyed the particular rapport they had, in all its freedom and intensity. Anne had never had children, and although regret is too strong a word—Anne was not a person who made concessions to emotions like regret—I knew that in her relationship with Xavier she was finding something she had not experienced elsewhere.

And in truth, I was delighted by the interest that Anne had taken in Xavier, there were even moments when I believed it was one of the most important things to come out of our extended collaboration. Xavier had always been a little adrift, excessively sensitive and easily buffeted by feeling, privately we worried that he was too porous for his own good. Tomas in particular felt that Xavier should be made to stand on his own two feet, that he was too easily dissuaded and discouraged, when it came to Xavier he was prone to speaking of *backbone* and *resilience*, things he evidently felt Xavier had not acquired earlier in life. But that night at the restaurant, as I watched Anne gather Xavier to her, in the face of Josie's irritation and to the amusement of the entire table, I wondered if after all he might pass through the world as he was, rather than as we feared he needed to be.

In any case, Anne seemed only to grow more attached to Xavier by the day, and I thought that even Tomas was beginning to realize that Xavier was more than capable of applying himself, and that the very things that worried him—Xavier's susceptibility to feeling, his porousness to those around him—might in fact be the things that allowed him to pursue the life he wished to lead. Now, as the three of us sat around the table, Tomas turned to look at Xavier and said, And let's toast you as well, Xavier. You're doing so well in this new position with Anne and we're both very proud of you. You're finding your feet. Xavier blushed, although he pretended that he did not require Tomas's approval, I knew that it meant a great deal to him. The two were not as close as Xavier and I were, but at times I felt that Xavier desired his approval more than mine, precisely because it was so often withheld. Everything he did was directed at Tomas, everything he did was a message for his father.

Xavier took a sip and lowered his glass a little nervously. He then said that Anne had offered him a position as an AD on the film she would begin shooting in the spring, her first. It would be concurrent with the final semester of his master's degree, at the same time that he would need to be completing his thesis, so he had decided to defer for a semester, possibly a full year, depending on how things went. I could see the wariness begin to come down across Tomas's face, like a curtain falling, although I didn't see any problem with Xavier's deferring a semester or two and said so at once. The work he's doing with Anne will open so many doors, I said. And it's not nothing to have a credit, at his age.

The waiter had arrived with our food and Tomas did not immediately reply. Hamburger and fries for Xavier, he always ordered hamburger and fries at this restaurant. What difference does it make whether he graduates this semester or next? I said once the waiter had gone. I looked at Xavier but his eyes were on Tomas, his face tense and uncertain, he seemed oddly reluctant to look at me. Tomas took a bite of food and wiped his mouth. Don't you think, Tomas? I said impatiently. He continued chewing, slowly and deliberately, as if mastication were the most important thing in the world to him, more important than our child and his happiness, for example. At last, he spoke. I'm in favor of you finishing the degree, he said gazing steadily at Xavier. Follow-through, he said as I sat back in exasperation, Xavier, you know how I feel about follow-through.

Tomas, I said, and I reached out and took Xavier's hand reassuringly. Xavier lowered his head and fiddled with his napkin, the kind of behavior that I knew would only further irritate Tomas. It's only one semester. Tomas frowned at me, I knew he felt that I was too prone to defend what he called Xavier's lack of application, and I suspected that he knew I did so in part because in Xavier I saw my own weaknesses and tendencies. If I had not found my work, and if I had not been good at it, my life might have had the same weightlessness. But to my surprise, after a long pause, Tomas shrugged. Perhaps you're right, he said and now he smiled at Xavier. I meant what I said. I'm happy about everything that is happening for you, happy that Anne has taken you under her wing.

But Xavier did not seem all that reassured, in fact he seemed to grow even more tense, and then he suddenly said that there was something else he wished to discuss. The lease is up on my apartment, he said. And I don't know if it makes sense for me to renew it, not if I'm going to be working on this film and I'm going to be away from the city for weeks at a time. We both nodded, I had the sense that Tomas was already braced for whatever would come next. Xavier hesitated. I wondered if I could stay in the apartment, just for a couple of months. I know it's asking for a lot, he continued. But I would barely be there, the days will be long and I'll be working weekends, Anne says.

To my surprise, Tomas did not reply but turned to look at me. For a long and unexpected moment, my mind was empty, it seemed to contain nothing at all, I felt only an incredible blankness. I lifted my hand to my face, instantly Tomas took it in his own, his fingers warm against my skin. I turned to look at him and relief flooded through me, it was as if I had been given my cue, it was as if I had received my prompt. I turned to Xavier and said, Of course. I reached out with one hand, the other still firmly held by Tomas, and covered Xavier's hand with my own. He turned up his palm and wrapped his fingers around mine and we remained that way, the three of us, as I said to Xavier, You must stay for as long as you like, it's your home after all.

Xavier looked not at me but at Tomas, who nodded slowly as he released my hand. When would you move in? he asked. I still had my hand over Xavier's. I now removed it and reached for my glass. Xavier hesitated, and then said, I wondered if this weekend might be possible. This weekend? Tomas asked sharply. But the end of the month isn't for two more weeks. Yes, I know, Xavier said and he sat back in his chair, exhaling gently, a movement he often made, a nervous tic of his. But Anne has me in the city day and night. The commute is so long and I'm starting to feel exhausted, but at the same time I don't want to let Anne down.

I gazed uneasily at Tomas, who was again watching me. I gave a small shrug. He turned to Xavier. Xavier, we want to help you, he said. And then he paused. You know that I will be home all day working.

I won't be there, I promise, Xavier said eagerly. I have to get up at the crack of dawn and I'm usually out in the evenings, you won't even know I'm there.

We want to know you're there, I said. We don't want to be ships passing in the night. I could see that Tomas was considering asking Xavier for a little time to think about it, I could see that he would have preferred to discuss the matter with me alone, without Xavier present. I smiled brightly at Tomas, it made no difference to me whether Xavier moved in two weeks or that very evening. I had the sense that another conversation was taking place, buried somewhere beneath or within this one, the words muffled so that I alone couldn't hear them, the two of them had a complicated relationship, there was always something being negotiated between them.

You must move in whenever you like, I said to Xavier firmly. Tonight, if need be. Tomas's expression softened just a little, and I knew that he had made up his mind. This is a temporary solution, you understand? Xavier nodded. Yes, absolutely, I promise. And you'll finish your degree? Tomas asked. Do you mean in return for a place to stay? Xavier replied. His voice had turned hard and the question seemed designed to provoke, but then I saw that his face was somber and chastened and he seemed to be genuinely asking the question, as if determined only to meet expectation and fulfill his obligations. Tomas shook his head and did not respond.

We agreed that Xavier would move in Saturday morning. When we had finished our meal and stood outside the restaurant, I embraced Xavier, I held him tightly. I thought he made a quiet sound of surprise, but I must have imagined it, soon his arms tightened around me in return and he lowered his head so that it rested against mine. The soft press of his cheek. I remembered then what it was like to embrace him as a child, the animal scent of the skin at his neck, the feeling was overwhelming. I pushed him away and told him to go, go before I started to cry.

We watched him disappear in the direction of the subway. Tomas took my hand and turned me gently away. Do you think he's okay? I asked. I hope he's okay. We began walking back to the apartment. And you, Tomas asked lightly, how are you? I'm fine, I said. Good, even. We returned home and

Tomas asked if I wanted another drink before we went to bed. A drink for going to bed was how we thought of it. I said yes and I followed him into the kitchen, once I had hung up my coat and bag, once I had slipped off my shoes.

He poured out a whiskey and handed it to me. It'll be fine, I said and he nodded. We're reaching the end of the run. I'll need a distraction. This seemed to persuade him, I knew that it had been a matter of concern to him, how it would be for me to give up the play, to leave that world behind. He smiled and took my hand, stroking the skin gently. He looked at me and we touched glasses, two people in the middle of their lives, and then we went to bed.

8

Xavier's room was filled with random clutter that had accumulated over the years, objects that I couldn't remember acquiring and that had no obvious source. It now seemed odd to me, that we had taken our son's bedroom and so briskly converted it into what was essentially a spare bedroom, a place for visitors rather than family. What had been the hurry, when we had no need for this space, when we appeared to have used it as little more than a storeroom? Of Xavier's old things, there was no trace, we had boxed everything away.

I spent several days preparing the room for Xavier's arrival. I dusted and vacuumed and scrubbed, I washed the linen and made the bed. There was a bedside table and an armchair and little else, the furnishings somehow provisional. As I stood and tried to think what else he might need, I had a memory of the room in his adolescent years, a mess of dirty clothes and half-eaten sandwiches, a disorder that had irritated me to no end, but for which I now found myself nostalgic. During that period of his life, I had myself been living in too contingent a way, spendings weeks and months in interstitial spaces, too often away from home, it was the nature of the work I did. Now, I only wanted for Xavier to be comfortable, to save him from that feeling of precarity, I wanted him to feel as if he were welcome, as if there were space in the apartment for him, his presence in no way conditional.

When I was done with the bedroom I continued working, even when it was evident there was not much else to do. The apartment had never been so clean, so presentable. Like a showroom of our lives. Several times, I caught Tomas watching me as I went about the apartment, cleaning and tidying and then cleaning and tidying again. It's Xavier, Tomas said teasingly. There's no need to treat him like a stranger. Remember, we don't want him to stay forever, we must not let him get too comfortable. But I brushed the comment aside, Tomas was always saying things like that, it was part of the reason why his relationship with his son was, on occasion, subject to strain.

The buzzer rang on Saturday morning, at a surprisingly early hour. Tomas and I were drinking our first cups of coffee, and even though Xavier had said that he would be coming that morning, we still looked at each other in surprise. Tomas touched my shoulder reassuringly, although it wasn't clear whose worry he was assuaging, and then he pressed the buzzer. A few minutes later we heard the ding of the elevator arriving and then a knock at the door and when Tomas opened it, there stood Xavier.

For a moment we stared at him, and then at the towering pile of bags and suitcases beside him. Neither of us moved to let Xavier in, neither of us said anything. But then Tomas seemed to shake himself out of his stupor, he reached forward to pick up one of the bags and together they began carrying Xavier's things into his old bedroom. I had placed a fresh set of towels on the newly made bed, as you might do for a friend or distant relative, visiting for the night. But as I watched Xavier and Tomas transfer the many boxes and cases into the apartment, I understood for the first time that this was not a question of someone staying for a month or even two, this was something else altogether.

Loudly, I said that I would run down to the café and pick up some breakfast. I hurried down the corridor to the bedroom without waiting for either of them to respond, pulling on my clothing, applying lipstick and brushing my hair, I felt momentarily ashamed that Xavier had seen me in this state. Through the door, I could hear the sound of bags dropping to the floor, the front door opening and closing and then opening again. I heard Xavier call out to Tomas, the muffled noise of his reply, and although I couldn't make out the individual words, I could hear the sound of their camaraderie. It occurred to me that they had always done better when I wasn't there, in my absence they understood how to be with each other. I picked up my purse, my keys, when I finally emerged Xavier was returning to the elevator. There are a few more bags downstairs, he said. Tomas was silent and then said, as the elevator doors closed on Xavier, that there was some space in our basement storage unit.

He spoke as if he were only talking to himself. I stared at the collection of bags and boxes, none of which I recognized, all of which seemed to belong to a stranger. Is there enough space in his room? I asked Tomas and he shrugged and said we would figure it out, he was oddly sanguine. Are you okay? he asked and he touched my arm, I could feel his fingers slide over the bones in my elbow, the radius and the ulna, the tender intricacies of his concern. I was perplexed, and as he continued to stare at me, I felt mild impatience at his worry. Beneath, the pounding sound of my heart.

At that moment, the elevator doors opened and Xavier appeared again, with yet more bags, a framed poster, and now even Tomas exhaled a little before taking a box from Xavier and carrying it in. There were books, an electric kettle, and a potted plant in the box Tomas held, and I stared at the fronds erupting from his arms before I said that I was going, slipping out of the apartment.

As I walked down the street, I was suddenly overwhelmed by a newfound awareness of the life we had together, Tomas and me. It was one we had built over the course of our marriage, and it bore the texture of many shared intimacies and affinities, a weave so tight that it seemed impossible that it could accommodate another person. I entered the café and ordered, face still cold from the outside. I reminded myself that it had been, for so many years, the three of us. That our life, having contracted, could expand again. A departure, and now a return, that was the way to think of it. The woman held out my order, I took the bag and turned to go, I reminded myself again that this was only Xavier coming home.

I returned to the apartment with the bag of pastries, face

recomposed. When I pushed the door of the apartment open, I found that Xavier's bags and cases had been neatly placed in his bedroom and the door closed. Tomas and Xavier were sitting in the kitchen. Xavier was speaking quickly, as if he were relating something of great personal importance, while Tomas was nodding, apparently in sympathy, they appeared so intimate that I took an involuntary step back. I couldn't remember the last time I had seen them speaking in this way, the last time it had felt as if there was something Xavier wanted, urgently, to convey to his father.

They sat up when I entered. Xavier's face grew suddenly flushed, while Tomas's face remained studiously blank. Is everything okay? I asked and they both nodded. I turned away and took out plates, glasses, cutlery, I busied myself with the objects available to me. When I looked back they had moved apart a little and the sense I'd had of interrupting thickened into something else, and I had the thought that perhaps now, perhaps this time, the relationship between them would change and certain things would at last be resolved. I sat down at the table with them and poured coffee, I set out the pastries on the plate, the same breakfast we'd always had, ever since Xavier was a child.

Tomas took a croissant and began breaking it into pieces that he then dipped into his coffee. He ate with steady and controlled gusto, his wants always correctly tempered, never too much, never too little. Xavier got to his feet, he said that he wasn't hungry and that in any case he needed to go, Anne needed him. I looked up, a little bewildered and also, I realized, disappointed. On a Saturday? At this hour? I asked. He shrugged and then said that he had meant it when he said that he would be out of the apartment most days, that we would barely know he was here. There was an edge to his voice that I couldn't fully decipher, and I said again that we were so happy he was here, both of us, that he must stay as long as he needed.

As Xavier started to pull his coat on, I gave Tomas a look of sudden and vicious irritation, for a brief moment I could not bear the sight of him, eating with such healthy appetite. I began putting the pastries back into the bag and then held it out to Xavier. Take these, I said. You can share them with Anne. Doesn't she expect you to pick up breakfast? He stared at the bag and gave me a small, conspiratorial smile as he took it and reached for his coat. She does, he said. How did you know? And I reminded him that I had known Anne for a long time. Not in the way I do, he said wryly. I squeezed his hand and said, I've seen her with her assistants, and he gave another little smile. He said he wouldn't be back until late, and I said to text us, we would be getting dinner after the show as usual. He nodded and then he picked up the keys that until that moment had been sitting in the middle of the table. His fingers closing over the set. Don't lose them, Tomas said. They're our only spares. I won't, Xavier said.

And then he was gone. The kitchen suddenly felt empty. Tomas indicated the chair beside him, only recently vacated by Xavier, and I sat down with my coffee. I glanced restlessly around me, Xavier had left his scarf on the counter. How on earth did you fit all that stuff into his room? I asked. Tomas shrugged. There's barely enough space for him to move, he said. I'll help him take some of it down to the basement tomorrow. But he was insistent that we get everything into his bedroom, he didn't want to leave his things in the hall or the living room, he was quite scrupulous in that regard. Tomas looked at me. He is trying, he said. I nodded and picked up the scarf on the counter, Xavier's scarf.

I kneaded the soft material in my hand, I examined the tag, an expensive brand. It must have been a gift, possibly from Anne, it didn't seem like the kind of thing that Xavier would have chosen—too conservative, almost middle-aged in its style. And yet the material was pilled and worn with use, and I now recalled that I had seen Xavier wearing the scarf before, many times in fact, the memories collating in my mind and in my vision, thrown over his shoulder, puddled on a chair at a restaurant. A hand lingering and then tightening. How had I not recognized it earlier? When I scanned the images in my head, I couldn't really place them, they were oddly detached from context, from one angle their integrity appeared perfect, emerging whole and unbidden, and yet from another angle they appeared composed, almost fabricated, as if they might dissolve beneath the pressure of close examination.

I set the scarf down and rose to my feet. I think I'm going back to bed, I said. I had a matinee and an evening performance, I shouldn't have gotten up so early. Tomas reached for and stroked my hand. Can you rest for the morning? he asked. And I nodded. As I retreated down the hall to the bedroom, I passed Xavier's bedroom and slowed, enough to see the piles of bags and cases. He had emptied the contents of one duffel bag onto the bed, perhaps in order to find a change of clothes, and now his shirts and sweaters and trousers lay tumbled out on the surface of the bed, strangely intimate in their disarray. I thought again of the scarf he had left in the kitchen, I wondered if he would be cold. His throat exposed. I continued down the hall, I thought the apartment was quiet, quieter than I could ever remember it being, so quiet that all I could hear was silence.

We soon developed a routine, a way of being together again. A new constellation of old parts. We always woke on the early side, Tomas and I, we were now old enough that it no longer seemed possible to stay in bed very long, even when we had nothing in particular to do, no meetings or deadlines, even when we had returned home late and gone to bed even later—even then we awoke no later than six or seven. But to our surprise, it was the same with Xavier, often he was already up when we emerged from the bedroom, often he had turned on the coffee machine and was pulling on his coat to go out to the café to get some pastries or the egg sandwich that he now liked to eat for breakfast, and which I had learned to get for him when it was my turn to go out in the mornings.

Then he would return to the apartment and lay out the food and pour cups of coffee, and the thing that was surprising to us—surprising at least to me—was the naturalness with which he did this, as if at some point he had learned how to live a life, to look after himself and other people. It did not seem in any way performed for our benefit, it did not seem as if he were trying to convince us that he was a responsible person, that it had not been a mistake to let him move back home. He cleaned up after himself, washing the dishes and running the laundry, I began to wonder who had instructed him in this way. It was not me, it was not Tomas who had taught him how to cook an omelet when he came in late from work, to hang up his coat rather than toss it over a chair, to sometimes buy flowers and arrange them in a vase with more care than I, for example, would have been capable of.

He was changed, he had grown and matured in so many ways, and there were moments when I could see that Tomas was feeling no small pride in this transformation, and when I felt the same. In truth, it was not exactly like having our child back home again, it was like having some ideal version of him returned, altered in all the ways we had hoped. As the days passed, I realized how little continuity there was between the child or even the young man I remembered and the person now living with us. He was like a familiar stranger, someone you have known for a very long time but at a distance, or perhaps someone you knew long ago, for a brief but intense period, so that the familiarity was always mitigated, always compromised, always a little uncanny.

This was, perhaps, what it meant to have a child grow up. That distance finally achieved, in itself a kind of necessary estrangement. Oddly, despite the happiness that settled into our reconstituted household—and I felt certain that it was happiness—I did not think that Xavier quite felt himself to be at home. He seemed in every respect comfortable, not simply in physical or material terms, but existentially—he had somehow become a person who was always at home, no matter where he was in the world. It was something about working with Anne, perhaps, that had given him a certain amount of confidence but had also shown him how critical it was to adapt and be responsive, that to be as other people wanted you to be was fundamental to getting ahead in the world. But although Xavier was so evidently at home, he did not behave as if he were actually in his own home, he never inhabited the space as someone who had previously inhabited the space might do.

Sometimes I would see him looking for something in the kitchen, opening drawers and cabinets, and he would appear exactly like someone in a vacation rental, the way he moved through the space was as if he had no memory of having been there. I would ask him what he was looking for—a bread knife, a new roll of paper towels, the olive oil—and I would tell him where it was—the second drawer, inside the pantry, the cabinet on the right, where it always is—and I would watch as he carefully scanned the drawers, finding the right one, pulling it out as if he had not already done so hundreds or even thousands of times, as if he had not done it for his entire life. He would take out the knife, and then he would cut the bread as if the blade were new to him, and it was as if he had forgotten that he had ever lived here.

I admit the effect was a little disquieting, there could be moments of sudden vertigo, when he seemed to bend the space of the apartment toward him, so that it was not Xavier but the apartment itself that seemed subtly wrong. A warping in the very architecture of the place. But mostly, mostly I was delighted by Xavier's presence in the apartment, it was a joy to sit down to breakfast with him in the morning. True to his word, he was rarely there apart from that first meal of the day, leaving the apartment shortly after breakfast and returning a little before midnight, so that I would worry about whether he was getting enough sleep, I would worry about his health. I would miss him on the mornings when he had to leave the apartment so early that we did not see him, and I waited at night for him to return.

Perhaps I wanted more. He made no claim upon the space, during the day and into the evening it was possible to forget that he was staying with us, or that anything in the composition of the apartment had changed. The scarf he had left on the counter the morning he arrived was an unusual occurrence, on the whole the communal spaces of the apartment bore no trace of his presence. At times I would go in, ostensibly to empty the garbage or to leave fresh linen on the bed, playing the part of the diligent mother, but really to reassure myself that he was actually staying with us, that it wasn't a figment of my imagination but that it was real, real, materially real.

Within too, the room was surprisingly tidy, the clothes always neatly folded away in the bureau or hung up in the closet, there were never socks or underpants on the floor, there were never empty glasses or coffee cups accumulating on the bedside table, the books were neatly stacked, although also never disturbed, the sequence always the same—Montaigne, Brecht, Bergman screenplays, I traced my finger down the spines. I had always thought of Xavier as a voracious reader, as a child he was never without a book, although that might have been out of necessity as much as natural inclination, there were long periods of his childhood when he was waiting, in a dressing room, alone in the apartment, so that in some ways when I looked back on his childhood, he was at once there but also not there. Or perhaps it was that I was at once there but also not there, as if Xavier's childhood had taken place in my vicinity, with the details somehow escaping me.

But one thing I did remember, one thing I could recall distinctly, was the reading, the small child always carrying a book, the small child always a little removed into another world, his mind and heart elsewhere. These days, I never saw Xavier with a book, another way in which he had changed. One morning, in a sudden fit of nostalgia, I asked him why he no longer seemed to read. He stared at me, his face at once startled and blank, as if he had been caught off guard, as if the question were freighted in some way. Beneath the blankness I could see his mind at work, a series of rapid calculations, I understood that he had experienced the question as a criticism, even an accusation of sorts. The moment seemed to extend, I observed its viscous spread. I regretted having asked the question and was about to speak, to tell him never mind, when he cleared his throat and said that Anne had been keeping him busy, the one thing he regretted about the job was that he no longer had time to read. I remember thinking the phrase was odd, too generic for intimate conversation, but I only nodded and changed the subject, I left it at that. But even as we moved on to other matters, I could see that he remained preoccupied by the exchange, he sat at the kitchen table and he made conversation but I could see his mind whirring.

Soon after, perhaps even the same day, new books began to accumulate in his room, the titles of which were unfamiliar to me, philosophy and theory books, tomes about art history and biology, difficult books that I never once saw him read, and never once heard him discuss, but that seemed to accumulate at a spectacular rate inside his room. They remained there, and I would not have known about them except for the fact that I did, at least on occasion, continue to go into his room. There was always a plausible reason for doing so. The space remained as tidy as before, the bed always made, the shoes always neatly ranged against the wall, the only difference was in the growing piles of books. The other detail that I noticed was that the order of the books was always changing, as if each day he was sifting through and shuffling them, although to what end, for what purpose, that I could not discern.

9

Of course, I did not share this with Tomas. It would have sounded absurd—to say that Xavier was acquiring books but not reading them, to point out that the order of the books as they accumulated always seemed to be changing, even as we never actually saw Xavier reading— the words were ludicrous, too ludicrous to be spoken aloud, or even whispered inside a thought, at times I wondered if I was imagining it. I knew that if I told this to Tomas, I would see the crease appear in his forehead, the crease that meant he was once again worried, that my way of being was causing him concern.

One morning, we woke to discover that Xavier had

already left the apartment, but not before fetching and leaving a bag of pastries, I was reminded again of what a model son he had become. Tomas and I sat in the kitchen and had our breakfast. He poured more coffee and then carefully examined the plate of pastries in the center of the table. This act of contemplation was unbelievably slow, although Tomas was always deliberate in his choices, this was nothing new. Still, how interesting could the decision be? It was the same selection as always. I felt restless, I thought because of Xavier's absence, the morning was exactly as it used to be, before his return, but also completely transformed.

Tomas carefully extracted a Danish, examined its perimeter, and took a bite before speaking. It's quiet this morning, he said as he swallowed. Although it's not much louder when Xavier is actually in the apartment. Sometimes I listen, so that I can hear him when he comes home late at night, the sound of the key in the lock. He took another bite of the Danish and continued. Or when he goes into the kitchen, I listen to see if he's getting a drink, I wait for the sound of the tap, the thud of a glass set down on the counter. I stared at Tomas, he spoke with such tenderness, such attention. I had an image of him, pressing a glass to the wall, the empty glass from the kitchen even, it was so perturbing that I turned away from the image at once, as if swiftly closing a door.

There was a sudden distance between us, the barrier of that door. Who would have thought? Tomas said, and there was a quality of wonderment to the way he spoke. He did not seem as if he could grow to be so quiet, so very—he paused. Discreet.

Perhaps it means he's not really comfortable here, I said.

Tomas looked at me thoughtfully, then asked if I thought we should extend some greater accommodation to Xavier, if we should encourage him to make himself further at home. You know that first day when he moved in, he said, you reacted rather badly, do you remember? You ran out of the apartment as if the very sight of him standing in the hall made you uneasy.

His gaze felt heavy on me, so that I could feel its weight pressing on the surface of my skin, and I shook my head as if to evade its scrutiny. In fact, Tomas continued, Xavier asked me if after all it was a bad idea, if it would be better if he left, he said that Anne had offered him the spare room in her apartment. I reassured him, of course. But if you're wondering why he's behaving so cautiously, it's possibly because of this. As he spoke, I could tell that his mind had been turning over these thoughts for some time. He gazed at me for a little longer, and then leaned forward and said in a voice that was too quiet and too low and that flowed toward me too rapidly, Your approval means a great deal to him. I can tell him again that he's more than welcome, that we are delighted to have him in the apartment. But it means very little coming from me. The person he wants to hear from is you.

I stared at Tomas. Was this even the case, was this in any way true? Wasn't it Tomas whose approval he always sought, Tomas whose rejection he feared? I pressed my hands together, palms moist. I've told him many times how happy I am that he is here. And I am, I repeated, I am. The words, entirely robust in my head, sounded weak and ineffectual as I spoke them, as if they had been hollowed out. Tomas rubbed his eye with his thumb, slowly and methodically, the movement unsettled me further, he pressed his thumb deeper and deeper into the socket in a way that was unfamiliar to me, both the movement and its coarseness. Stop, I said. Stop. My voice was louder than I had intended. He looked at me with surprise. His hand dropped down to his lap. The eye was bloodshot, the skin around it blotchy, he had done it to himself and for no good reason. I had something in my eye, he said calmly. You've made it worse, I said and he gave a bland little shrug. Yes, he said, I suppose I have. His appearance was now a little deranged, with that single bloodshot eye, but when he spoke his voice was calm as always.

Things are different now that Xavier is back, he said, but that's not a bad thing. We are becoming too settled in our ways, in all these little rituals—and here he gestured to the breakfast laid out before us, the cups and the plates and the food—it's in all these little rituals that people grow old without noticing. I stared at the table, which I had set, and which appeared suddenly diminished and absurd. He had dismissed it with such ease—it being not simply the table, not even just the hand that had set out the cups and plates and saucers, but also the habits that had formed our marriage, and by extension, the life we had built together.

I thought you liked the rituals, I said. And I rose from the table abruptly. I could no longer remember how the ritual of the breakfast had begun, how we came to sit down together in this way every morning, rather than going our separate ways. The rituals, I said, and I spoke with my back to him so that my face was concealed, in that moment I did not trust myself. You told me they had a purpose. That they were a pleasure. My voice sounded grating to my own ears, full of unpleasant need. I turned at last to look at him. Tomas took another bite of his Danish, wiped his mouth with the napkin I had laid out earlier. It's only breakfast, he said wearily. He poured the last of the coffee into his cup and then stood to refill the kettle. And that's not the point. The point is that we're lucky to have him here, he said. Don't you think?

I could see he wasn't waiting for me to respond, he came and stood beside me and although he was looking into my face, his mind was elsewhere, it had become slippery as a fish. His face brightened and then he went to rinse his cup. I have been thinking that we should do more for Xavier, he said in a voice that was too smooth, that had a little more velocity than usual. The other day he complained that his back was hurting, he spends so much time working from his bed, he doesn't have a proper place to do his work.

Work? I wondered aloud. What do you mean? What kind of work?

His writing, Tomas explained patiently, as if I should have known, as if this were some long-standing dream or ambition on Xavier's part. But I had never heard him mention it, I could not recall a time when it had come up in conversation, this was not something I knew. He's having difficulty making the time, Tomas continued, Anne is demanding, as you know. But I've been encouraging him to prioritize his own work. I said that we could put a desk in the living room, perhaps some more shelving. He has so many books, he said, and I found myself nodding, this at least was true, I was glad Tomas had noticed, he did have so many books. I was about to ask him if he had ever actually seen Xavier reading any of the books, but he pressed on, I could see he had the bit between his teeth. In fact, I meant to tell you, I ordered a desk, it should arrive later this week, let me show you—and he pulled out his phone.

I glanced at the image on his screen. You bought this? I asked, not a little stupefied. I took the phone from him and zoomed in on the image. The desk was enormous, a swooping thing of glass and metal, I couldn't begin to understand the purchase. Xavier chose it and I thought, why not? Tomas said a little sheepishly. We can easily clear some space. It doesn't exactly fit into the general décor of the apartment, but that's almost the point, it's something that he chose for himself. It's expensive, I said, and now he looked at me in surprise, before replying with some hesitation, It's not as if we can't afford it, and then he gestured around the kitchen, around the apartment, even down at the clothes I was wearing. I felt the color rise in my face, it was true I spent too much money on clothes, true I liked things that were beautiful and unnecessarily expensive.

I immediately felt parsimonious and unkind. Why would I wish to withhold this from my son, where did this instinct come from? He took the phone from me and gently said, Change is good, it's how we keep from growing old. I stared at him, I had never heard this wheedling tone, slick with dishonesty and cliché, I had never heard him speak in language that was so secondhand. I realized that I was being handled by Tomas. This was not in and of itself so unusual, but there was a desperation, a shoddiness, to the way it was being done that was new.

You like having him here, I said, and I realized that the statement came as a surprise to both of us. He shrugged. At first, I didn't know how it would go, he conceded, I didn't know how it would affect you. But in truth, he hurried on, as he saw me begin to protest against the insinuation, the substance of which he seemed incapable of declaring, in truth, it's no inconvenience, it's almost entirely a pleasure. And I wish he were here more often—even right now, for example, it would be fun if he was here, don't you think? Nicer, even?

And as he stared at me, I found it impossible to disagree. It had been a long time since I had been with Tomas and longed for the company of others, but at that moment I would have welcomed the presence of someone else, anyone else. Hastily, I began to clear the table. The air felt thick, pregnant with presence. There was something new between us, something that needed to be tempered, that required a solvent of some kind. Something that needed to be cut back, with all the violence those words implied.

Later that week, as Tomas had promised, the desk arrived. I watched as the deliverymen carried it up the stairs—it was too large to fit inside the elevator, even disassembled—and then through the front door and into the apartment. They asked Tomas where he wanted it and he pointed to a space that he had cleared, along the wall and below the large window, so that Xavier would have a view out onto the city as he worked. I had to admit that it would make an ideal space for writing, although I also could not imagine Xavier sitting at the desk, doing whatever it was he did when he was working. To me his writing was a little like his reading— the material evidence of it accumulated by the day, in the form of this desk, those books, and yet I was never able to catch him in the act of doing either.

It appeared Tomas had also ordered one of those ergonomically designed office chairs, I watched as the deliverymen carried it in and unwrapped the many layers of foam and plastic in which it had been mummified. It's very large, I murmured to Tomas, who answered quietly that he needed a new chair anyway, and he would use it once Xavier moved on. And the desk? I asked, to which Tomas did not reply, perhaps even he was daunted by the sight of this enormous slab of glass, a piece of furniture so ostentatious and so fundamentally obtrusive it seemed impossible to reconcile with any actual person's life.

But within a matter of days, the desk barely gave pause, Xavier brought out the books from his bedroom and placed them in neat stacks on the desk, obscuring its aggressive simplicity, its cloying transparency. And although I mostly saw Xavier at the desk at odd hours—late at night or early in the morning—I had to admit that the desk, his occasional presence at it, had opened up the apartment, we seemed to move through it more freely, the air circulating more regularly, the space had changed again in some subtle way I couldn't define.

Sometimes, on the weekends, Xavier would work at his desk—despite some prodding on my part he wouldn't tell me what he was writing, although at one point Tomas alluded to a play, without saying anything further—and although Tomas would have already spent the week working, and although in general he would always be careful to take the weekends off, in order to forestall sinking too deeply into the soup of his own thoughts and losing the clarity he required to write, despite this Tomas would retreat to his study, where he would also spend the day at his desk, occasionally emerging for tea or coffee, for something to eat, in order to check in with Xavier and see how his work was going. I realized that this companionable routine—the two of them, ensconced in the individual worlds that they were creating, and yet working in synchronization—was bringing Tomas considerable happiness, it was even possible that this was the happiest he had ever been in his working life, which had always been fraught, full of private agonies and uncertainties that he was not always able to share, lest it alter the delicate balance of the internal arguments, themes, structures he was forming in his head.

Watching him, I realized that he had craved this communion, perhaps without even understanding it, to know that Xavier was at work at his desk, while he himself was also at work in his study, it was so simple a thing I almost laughed. I had never before thought of Tomas as unhappy— and if you had asked me, I would have said that of the two of us, he was the happier, the one more naturally inclined to contentment—and yet I now realized that if he had not been unhappy, he had not been happy either, not in the way he seemed to be now. He was invigorated by Xavier's presence in the apartment, the whole of his being energized, as if he had suddenly shed years. He behaved like a man who had things to look forward to, and it was only in that moment, I suppose, that I understood how limited it had become for him, the idea of our own future together, nothing more than a downward slope into old age.

It might have been that I was aware of it before he was. But it was undeniable, over the days that followed I saw that he moved through the apartment with more vigor, his posture a little more upright and buoyant. I noticed that he began to pick up little things when he was out, cheese, fruit, bottles of wine, purchasing more than he and I could ever consume on our own. He would leave these things in the kitchen and tell Xavier to help himself, although he did not need very much encouragement, in this respect at least he remained the same as in his teenage years, raiding the refrigerator every night upon his return home, although on the other hand again, in the morning the dishes were always washed and dry on the rack. But it was not the fact that Tomas was clearly purchasing these little extravagances for Xavier that was notable. It was that he seemed to have a newfound pleasure in life, as if appetites he had forgotten or not experienced for many years had now suddenly returned.

If I hadn't been observing Tomas so closely, if I wasn't so certain of what was behind this change in manner, I would have assumed he was having an affair. In fact, the behavior was not so vastly different—a more profligate manner, a loosening of the old habits and constraints that had drawn the boundary around his person and made him who he was. I knew that it was simply the presence of youth in the apartment, the reminder that life radiated outward, when for so long it had been concentrated inward, slowly reducing in scale if not intensity. But increases of appetite can be disquieting, it is strange to see a person you have known for so long newly hungry, and in so many ways.

And I suppose in that sudden mood of expansiveness, I had the feeling or suspicion or revelation that our life together—it hadn't been enough. For so many years there had been the tacit understanding that I contained the threat to the marriage, that it was housed inside me. And for all those years I had tamped down every impulse to stray, I had lived inside a straitjacket of my own devising, and I had remained true. But in the end, he was the first to tire of the marriage, he was the first to look outside, to open the door and taste the fresh and free air. He was the first, and he was always bound to be the first, because of course I needed him, I needed Tomas, much more than he needed me, and this had always been the case, whether I was able to admit it or not. It was him, and it was always going to be him.

10

ONE MONTH AFTER HE MOVED INTO THE APARTMENT
and only a few weeks before the end of the play's run,
Xavier asked if he could bring a friend to stay. He asked
Tomas, rather than me, and Tomas then asked me, on Xavier's behalf. And so I did not know the precise manner in
which the original request was made, the nature of the conversation between them. What I was told was that Xavier
had a friend, who needed a place to stay, because of the va-
garies of a lease or roommate, the reason was at once wholly
plausible and completely vague.

When I pressed Tomas, he was furtive in a way that was
increasingly familiar, and I did not pursue the matter any

further. By this point, it was understood that Xavier would be living with us for as long as he pleased. We had reached an equilibrium, so that it was easy to imagine the arrangement continuing not just for months but for years. There was naturally a shift in the balance of power, which was felt by all of us. It was never commented upon, but it was nonetheless palpable, the shift being entirely in Xavier's favor.

Because it had become apparent that we now desired it more than Xavier did—we being Tomas and I, and it being the situation, for the situation to prolong itself indefinitely, to take on a life of its own. Certainly, there were all the material things we were able to provide, a place to sleep and stay rent free, and then the food, the bills, the little envelopes of money that were left on the console by the door. But as the weeks passed, those things did not seem to matter in quite the same way, and the gratitude Xavier expressed started to feel a little rote, the conversion from the material to the emotional never as frictionless as hoped, value always being shed along the way. Perhaps we then became a little more extravagant in the gestures that we made, the envelopes growing thicker and heavier, the gifts increasing in frequency.

Evidently sensing this—our desire to please, and perhaps even more, for continuance, we were only trying to maintain the equilibrium that we had attained—Xavier made his demand, he asked Tomas if Hana could come to stay, although I did not know her name until later, until her actual arrival. The precise nature of the relationship between Xavier and this young woman, this friend, was not explained to me, although I had the sense that I'd heard her name before, some mention of knowing each other through school. Again, it all felt plausible and vague, down to the very fact of Hana herself.

But certain things became clear when she arrived the following night with Xavier. It was nearing midnight, and we were in the living room having a last drink before bed. I was calm, I didn't have a show the following day and I had said to Tomas that we could have one more and he agreed. Xavier was not home, although that was not surprising. I was about to get up and go to bed when there was a sound at the door, somehow more clatter than usual, and we raised our heads in alarm, although also, I saw it clearly in Tomas's face, with some anticipation. We remained frozen in our armchairs as we heard them enter the apartment, heard Xavier call out hello, as if in warning, so that we could be prepared, for whatever it was that was coming.

We're in here, Tomas said, and slowly we rose to our feet. Then they appeared in the doorway, Xavier and Hana. She was leaning heavily on his arm, although she did not appear in any way inebriated, and while I could understand her desire to be close to him—he was the kind of person people wanted to be close to, I knew this to be true—it was the fact of their mutual inclination that gave me pause. It was clear from a single glance that Xavier was equally drawn to her, they were so strongly united in their youth and general appearance that there was a logic to the way they cleaved together. If anything, as we stared at them, I thought I sensed in Hana a curiosity and a hunger that extended beyond Xavier, that did not stop—that did not even perhaps begin—with him, and that could never be satisfied by his person alone.

She looked at Tomas, and then she looked at me, and as she stepped forward with her hand extended, because in fact she had wonderful manners, everything about her was perfect, I watched her with great trepidation. She was not exactly beautiful, her face did not have the alarming symmetry of Xavier's face for example, her eyes were not so large and startling, nor did she possess the placidity of great beauty. Was it surprising to us that she was the one Xavier was bringing home? Only in the sense that it showed he had greater imagination than either of us had given him credit for, we had always expected him to show up with some stereotype or another, a composite of hair and lips and eyes, rather than with this strange and unsettling creature, more genuinely alluring.

Tomas took her hand in his, his smile already an embarrassment to us both. She turned next to me, and I took her hand in mine—her skin smooth and her grip so light as to be an act of aggression, it left me with the sensation that I was holding on to nothing. She made it so that I was the one who was grasping, the one who was seeking more than was being given, and as I released her hand, I wondered what this evasive physicality boded for Xavier. Although it was possible that he experienced it not as evasion, but rather as a kind of yielding. My smile had grown stiff over the course of this brief interaction, so that as she stepped back and I turned away, I had the impression that I had been grimacing, that I had almost been baring my teeth.

Hana. I couldn't remember the moment when she introduced herself, if she had spoken her name or if it had been Xavier, such was the extent of my disorientation. The name meant flower in Japanese, but also bliss in Arabic, a name that had many meanings in many different places. She did not seem too bothered by my behavior, although I noted that she rapidly retreated to Xavier, who wrapped his arm around her shoulders and held her close. I found it absurd that he had not told us exactly who she was to him, considering that he seemed unable to keep from touching her, considering that it was already obvious where and with whom she would be sleeping that evening. I watched them and I remembered what it had been like, to have a body that other people desired in so helpless a fashion.

I looked at Tomas, who had what I can only describe as a stupidly pleased expression on his face as he gazed at Xavier and Hana. I said loudly that it was late and that I would be going to bed, but before I could turn to go Hana told me that she was a great admirer of my work, shaking off Xavier's arm and reaching for my hands, again that strange and ghostly touch. She gave a little laugh and said, I don't mean to make you uncomfortable, and I thought to myself that was exactly what she was trying to do. But I thought it best to say it at once, she continued, *Parts of Speech* was so important to me. To see someone who looked like me on the screen. You have no idea what it meant.

I smiled a little nervously, her words appeared to be sincere, that is to say I didn't think they were mere manipulation, although I already knew she was more than capable of such a thing. It occurred to me that I was about to be trapped in my own home. *Important* and *great admirer* were words so generic as to mean nothing at all, to be almost an affront, and how many times had I been told how much it meant to some person or another, seeing *someone who looked like me* onstage or on-screen. I gestured for help, but both Tomas and Xavier were looking at Hana with silent approval, as if this piece of meaningless flattery, this apparently intimate disclosure, were certain to endear her to me. But nobody wishes to be a monument, least of all me.

Their attention next turned to me, in order to observe the happy result of Hana's blandishments, to exclaim over how the two of us were going to get along beautifully, and to my surprise—I suppose because I have made a career of knowing what is expected of me, and delivering it, both as a woman and as an actor—I acquiesced.

You're very kind, I murmured, squeezing her hands. And I'm so happy that you're staying with us. I continued to hold her hands tightly, kneading them with my own, so that she winced a little in discomfort. Of course, I then squeezed them harder. Tell me what we can do, I said, and reluctantly released her hands and turned to look at Tomas. All of this, apart from the small moment of malice, performed for the benefit of someone other than myself. Tomas was frowning at me, he knew me too well not to have understood all the constituent parts of the exchange, and I made a little face at him before turning back to look at Hana, my smile very dazzling. I noted that I was a little taller than she was, although she wore heeled boots, almost as soon as I had the thought she straightened a little. Is there anything you need, anything at all we can do to make your stay more comfortable? I flinched, these words were wrong, I sounded like a hotel clerk, completely impersonal, I was tired and it was late. I tried again. We'll have plenty of time to talk, later, I said, and then, hopelessly flailing, added, There are towels in the closet, before turning and fleeing in the direction of the bedroom.

When I emerged from the bedroom the following morning, it was still very early. Tomas was asleep and the apartment was quiet, I was the first to wake. I had slept very soundly. Some part of me had been first stimulated and then exhausted by Hana's arrival, and the result was a deep sleep such as I had not enjoyed in months. I woke up in a good mood, without knowing why, and decided I would get up and make tea for Tomas, briefly I forgot that there was anyone staying with us.

Then I went into the kitchen and found Hana, sitting at the breakfast table. I stopped in the doorway and we stared at each other. There was a little gleam in her eye, she had succeeded in surprising me in my own home, she had scored a point. But then her features reassembled, she gave a small and hopeful smile and got to her feet and asked if she could make me a cup of tea, her manner so docile that I wondered if I'd been wrong, about the gleam in the eye and the exchange the night before. As she moved around, she was only a very young woman in a kitchen, making a cup of tea. Where is Xavier? I asked as she handed me the cup. Asleep, she said. It's early. But I get up early, on the whole. And how long have you known Xavier? I asked. Long enough, she said with a low and unembarrassed laugh, and I thought that after all I had been right, of course I had been, about the night before, about everything.

He's never mentioned you, I said flatly.

Oh really?

She spoke in a voice that was completely unconcerned, as if the fact said more about my relationship with Xavier than hers. I was a little unnerved and said that I was going for a walk, I took another sip and then put the tea down on the counter. She rose to her feet and stood close beside me, until I felt obliged to ask if she wished to join me, although I regretted the words as soon as they were spoken. She nodded eagerly and said she would just get dressed, and I went to the door to pull a coat on over my pajamas. When she emerged from Xavier's bedroom, dressed all in black, black sweater and black trousers and black boots, she glanced at me and asked if I was going out like that and I said that I was, that I always did. And she tilted her head a little and said that of course I could get away with it. Her voice was rueful and sycophantic once more, and I said shortly that at my age you could get away with a great deal.

She followed me out into the hall and we waited for the elevator in silence. By the time we emerged into the street, the silence had held for long enough that I wondered if we could continue this way indefinitely, to the café and back, I felt my heart lift a little with the hope. But almost as soon as the chill air hit our faces, she turned and said that she hoped she had not made me feel uncomfortable last night. I told her not to worry about it, and then asked how long she would be staying. Was it some issue with a lease? I asked. Xavier wasn't terribly clear. She blinked placidly and said, Things with Xavier are quite serious. She spoke with the blandness of utter confidence, and although her words were not an answer to the question I had asked, they also were, she had addressed the question behind the question, the one we both knew I had been asking.

Quite serious? But how? I said and I came to a stop in the middle of the sidewalk, my heart loud in my ears. She continued to move forward, so that I was obliged to hurry after her. What does that mean? I called out. We're seeing how things go, she said and began to walk even faster, so that I had to scurry simply in order to keep up, she was not looking at me but focused on the street ahead. We'll see, she said, and I placed my hand on her arm to stop her. She turned to face me. It's not clear to us how long Xavier will stay, I said, and she nodded and said that much depended on Anne, of course. No, I said, what I mean is that this—and I gestured around me, as if the air that circulated around us in some way represented the apartment itself, the bed she was sleeping in. Although in fact we were standing in the middle of the street. This is a temporary situation, I continued, who knows how long it will last before we drive one another crazy.

I laughed, too loud, because I felt as if I were betraying Xavier and because my words were so palpably false—hadn't we said, only the other day, that Xavier must stay for as long as he liked, hadn't Tomas just been musing on the possibility of purchasing the apartment next door and knocking a wall down, so that we might all continue to live together, for the, or at least one, foreseeable future—and because I was already aware, even as the words were spoken, that she also knew they were not true, and that this knowledge would not keep her from repeating what I had said to Xavier. Hana unsettled me, I reminded myself that it was the cost of having Xavier stay with us, we had to accommodate his life as it was, out in the world and beyond the confines of the family. For all my trepidation, I already knew that I would endure her if I had to, if that was the price that must be paid.

Now she pressed her hand upon my arm with that strange feathery touch of hers, and said, I know it's an adjustment. She spoke in a conspiratorial way, so that I immediately wondered what she meant by it, and what Xavier had said to her, she had already made herself both the barrier and the conduit between me and my child. I could see the café down the street, in a few minutes we would reach it. I turned to her and said, What do you mean? She gave a small smile, vain and self-satisfied, so that she revealed herself without meaning to. I know that your relationship has been volatile in the past, she said smoothly. This reconciliation means a great deal to Xavier. Try to understand—and here her feathery touch suddenly seemed to sprout claws, so that her grip on my arm was ferocious and I winced in pain and alarm— you are the most important person in his life, you must know how much you affect him.

We had reached the café and she opened the door and ushered me in, her hand still tight on my arm. He has such a little boy lost air to him, she said musingly. It's part of his appeal. Her voice was so light, so natural, had I ever met anyone so at ease? The noise in the café was unbearable, the voices of the customers loud as if they were speaking from the inside of my head. The individual sound of metal scraping on ceramic, a spoon turning inside a cup. Hana's voice cut through the cacophony, He needs to grow up, she said. And here she actually twisted my arm, leveraging her grip so that I was facing her and she could gaze directly into my face.

There had been an undercurrent of sympathy and tenderness in her voice, but when she turned to look at me what I mostly saw was rage. I took a step back, although what I was afraid of was not her. I don't know what you mean, I said in a low voice. There was never any reconciliation, because there was never any rupture, there has never been any estrangement between us. We're fine. We always have been. I tried to shake her hand off but her grip was strong, so that I had to move my arm viciously, if you were to go from appearance alone, you would have thought we were on the verge of having an altercation. She loosened her fingers a little but still did not remove her hand, instead she maneuvered me into the line, and in a calm and solicitous voice, she asked what we should order.

11

I DID NOT REPLY, AND WE STOOD IN TENSE SILENCE
until we reached the front of the line. Just as the woman
asked what we'd like, I had the memory or the sense that it
could have been Xavier rather than Hana, standing watch-
fully beside me as I placed my order. I found myself adding
more and more things, as if we were feeding a large group
of people, an extended family, I kept ordering so that I could
avoid this uncomfortable echo between Hana and Xavier,
Xavier and Hana, I needed the feeling to dissipate.

And I suppose I had no desire to speak to Hana either.
But she said nothing as she reached up to take the enormous
bags of food, which she then insisted on carrying back to

the apartment, as if I were in no state to perform the task myself, although what she believed my state to be was unclear. She made no further mention of the supposed reconciliation that had taken place between us, between Xavier and me, in fact she made no mention of Xavier at all. She had no reason to do so, she had achieved what she had set out to achieve, and if she did not directly refer to Xavier his presence was implicit in her manner, in her every gesture. I realized as we made our way back to the apartment that she was playing the role of the dutiful daughter-in-law, having met me only twelve hours earlier. I chafed at the part she made of me, the aging and difficult mother-in-law, she opened the door to the building for me, her arms full of food, the act ostensibly one of kindness, but in fact designed to make me feel helpless and incompetent.

By the time we had returned, although we were not gone for very long, both Xavier and Tomas were up and waiting for us, nearly at the door and with so much expectation in their faces. Hana gave one of her irritating little laughs and said as she gave Xavier a kiss, open and on the mouth, You're awake. I gave a little grimace of disgust, which she may or may not have seen. She moved smoothly into the kitchen with the bags and began taking out plates and cups and cutlery. She had been in the apartment for no time at all and yet she already knew where everything was, within minutes she had arranged the food on the table and was pouring coffee. I remained standing as Xavier and Tomas sat down, exclaiming over the food, although it was only the usual food, the same food from the same café that we ate every morning, just more of it.

I took my coat off and sat down. I heard Hana asking if anyone wanted eggs, it would be no trouble at all, and at that I rose again and said that I was tired and would go lie down. Tomas nodded and I heard Xavier say, She doesn't like breakfast, she never eats it. Although this was not true, it was not true at all. Why would he say such a thing, hadn't we always had breakfast together, all through his childhood? I retreated out of the kitchen and down the hall, I couldn't wait to get away. I closed the door to the bedroom. Even so, I could hear their voices, a chorus of good cheer. I sat down on the bed and stared up at the ceiling, I could picture the three of them sitting around the kitchen table, mouths stuffed with food that I had picked out and paid for, so happy in one another's company. I had needed, Tomas would explain to Hana, time to myself, and she would nod, a little open-mouthed.

What else would they say, now that I was no longer present? Their voices scratching inside my ear, termites eating away at wood. I wondered what Hana wanted, I knew she could not be solely motivated by her affection for Xavier.

There was more to Hana than her feeling for a man, an admission that made her grow in my mind, so that I had a vision of her sitting at the kitchen table, her body extending and expanding so that it occupied the entire room, and so that I also felt with her an unexpected but undeniable affinity. She was like me, more like me than I wanted to admit.

I recalled her words, *I know that your relationship has been volatile in the past.* But I didn't know what she meant, I didn't know what she was referring to, I had a good relationship with Xavier, after all he had chosen to come back home, he had chosen to live with us again. But it was also true that there were long periods when I did not seem to think of our relationship at all, when it was as if our relationship did not exist, it did not occupy any space in my mind. Was it normal for a mother to be so unreflective? When I thought about my relationship with Xavier, when I looked back upon it, my memory was alarmingly inconsistent and full of gaps, so that I could not really say how it had been, at various stages of his life, his childhood and adolescence. What little there was had a certain thinness, like clips spliced together and aged by way of a filter, none of it seemed like the record of events that had actually taken place.

Perhaps that pointed to an estrangement, a series of them in fact, the memory of which I had failed to retain, the fact of which I had not experienced. The voices in the kitchen grew a little louder, there was a crash—a sound like pans being dropped from some height into the sink—and then a laugh that I didn't recognize, I thought the voice belonged to Tomas, and yet I had never heard him laugh in this way before, the sound a little unhinged. Tomas was a man of exquisite control, the hectic laughter was extraordinarily jarring. But I too had lost my equilibrium, been seized by some fervor, insidious and overly proximate, I thought again of Hana's words, I tried to think, once more I tried to understand what she was referring to—had I not been a good mother to Xavier?

I recalled Tomas's trepidation when Xavier had asked if he could stay, all of it suddenly had new meaning. I stood up restlessly, I tried to reconstruct the sequence of events, which now began to warp in my memory, I was no longer certain of what had taken place. It had been at dinner, Xavier had asked if he could move in, he had been nervous, and the question had been—as it came out of his mouth and into my ears—fraught. I remembered my mind puzzling over it, why was the question so troubling, why had I not known how to respond, although I had responded, I had said yes, it had not even taken me very long to do so, I had been worried that Tomas would change his mind.

And yet I felt that if I pushed further, I would see that this moment—a brief flicker of doubt and nothing more, a sensation pressed downward and away—was only the symptom of something else altogether. But what? I now recalled the morning Xavier arrived, the twist of anxiety inside me, the panic that had surged up when the doorbell rang, when Tomas opened the door, when he appeared in the apartment. And Xavier's face—also stricken with apprehension, a mirror to my own, as we stared at each other we had both been feeling the same thing, a kind of wariness based on past experience, we had been trying in that moment to overcome our doubt, to move beyond some thing, some event, that had occurred in the past.

And Tomas—he had watched us cautiously, at the time I thought he was absorbed in helping Xavier carry his things in, at the time I thought that my inner turmoil had gone unnoticed, the convulsion of feeling undetected. But now I saw that he had been managing both of us, that he had been doing his utmost to orchestrate what I now understood was a rapprochement of sorts, from which it followed that there had been a rift or period of estrangement. And I realized that Xavier's arrival had in some way been anticipated by Tomas, that he had been waiting and planning for it. The happiness that had come upon him had not been a surprise, it had not been an unexpected outcome of this new living arrangement, that very happiness was what Tomas had, all this time, been seeking.

And I knew then that even as Tomas had moved from one of us to the other, his concern had really been with Xavier, he had wanted to protect him, and the force or person or event that he wanted to protect him from was me. About this I did not know how to feel, I could not move beyond the single realization—that the problem, the problem we had all been moving around, it was me.

She stayed, of course. Anne had gone on vacation, for at least a month, she said, the shoot had been pushed back and she needed the break. Xavier was now at home during the day, and as for Hana, she did not appear to have anywhere she needed to be, anywhere other than here with Xavier. We ceded the living room to the two of them, even I understood that they could not be expected to remain inside Xavier's small bedroom. They occupied the apartment with remarkable ease, bodies intertwined, as they lay on the sofa or sometimes on the floor. Their things too were no longer in any way contained, in fact it was a spectacular mess, their clothes and shoes on the carpet, on the chairs, their books and computers and other devices on the tables and shelves, every socket in the wall claimed.

The desk that Tomas had purchased for Xavier was now

mostly occupied by Hana, who crouched upon the chair in animal fashion, peering at her laptop, always working on some document, some text. They were like this for hours at a time, maintaining a calm and almost conspiratorial silence, Hana writing feverishly at the desk and Xavier lying on one of the sofas, eating a sandwich, flicking through his phone, sometimes reading a magazine, one of the many subscriptions that we kept. He was remarkably idle, he seemed to feel no shame at the example set by Hana's intractable focus, if anything it seemed to make him more committed to his indolence.

He had form in the matter, having passed his adolescent years in this exact pose. As I peered from the doorway, the image of Xavier lying on the sofa was deeply familiar, in the way of a daily memory and concern, we had worried about depression and the usual things parents fret about, so that those old emotions seemed to well inside me again. But at a second glance, the image of this person on the sofa again grew subtly different, in ways that I could not immediately identify and that did not have to do with either age or time. Its wrongness only seemed to grow and seep toward me, across the floor, into the memories I had, or thought I had, of Xavier's childhood and adolescence. As if nothing retained its integrity, nothing remained stable or untouched.

Was it any wonder that I didn't venture any further, that I didn't cross the threshold? It was not only me, I was not the only one to sense the cordon that had been drawn around the living room. Tomas now only entered under the guise of delivering trays of food and drink, he had taken to preparing elaborate plates, complicated libations, and bringing them in to Hana and Xavier, so that sometimes I would peer into the cavernous room and see them eating from the trays while Tomas cleared up around them like a waiter or butler of some kind, his manner strangely submissive, wholly altered.

One day, I found Tomas in the kitchen, preparing yet another tray of food, this time a plate of cheese and charcuterie, little dishes of olives and pickles, I watched as he took a bottle of champagne out of the refrigerator. I said in a quiet voice, Why are you doing this? It's better this way, he said. Otherwise, they'll be in the kitchen, they'll take it over as well. He set two glasses on the tray, humming some tune, and said happily, Can you imagine the mess? I stared at him, he wasn't answering my question at all. No, he said as he lifted the tray and made his way down the corridor to the living room, it's better this way. I trailed after him as he carried the tray, heavy with food and drink, into the living room. You can leave it there, Hana said from the desk, without turning to look at him. As if he were delivering room service at a hotel. I watched from the safety of the corridor as Tomas turned, his back rigid, and carefully set the tray down on the coffee table, his movements stiff so that I knew the strain of carrying the tray had been considerable.

A rattle of dishes, nothing close to a crash, as he lowered it to the table. Still, Hana turned with a look of fierce irritation, as if her focus had been unforgivably disturbed, and I heard Tomas murmur an apology. I saw his posture slump with humiliation, he suddenly looked like an old man. It did something to me, seeing him this way, and I felt a surge of wild anger. Xavier had been lying on the sofa and now he roused himself and sat up. He gave a sharp glance over the shoulder at Hana, it might have been a look of admonishment or warning, before turning the high beam of his smile upon Tomas. Champagne, he murmured. Wow. He picked up a clump of prosciutto with his fingers, shoving the meat into his mouth, plucking at an olive, he wiped his fingers on a napkin and then asked if there were any crackers.

Crackers, Tomas said blankly, as Xavier rose to his feet and picked up a flute of champagne and shook it in Hana's face with an insolent wiggle of the hips. She glanced at him and gave a single, dismissive shake of the head. Xavier shrugged and returned to the sofa. He drank down the champagne and looked up at Tomas. Yeah, he said slowly. Crackers. And though I could see the thought pass through Tomas's mind, the impulse to tell him to get it himself, the kind of thing he would have said to Xavier a thousand times in the past, he only stood very still for a moment before turning and shuffling out of the room. When had he started moving in this shambling way? As he came toward me, I could see that he was avoiding eye contact, that he didn't want me to ask him what on earth he was doing, how he could allow them to speak to him in this manner. Quickly, he shoved past me and into the kitchen.

I followed and stood before him so that he could not evade me. What is happening? I asked in a low voice. I pointed in the direction of the living room, of Hana and Xavier. Why do you allow them to treat you like this? To speak as if you're the help? I gestured at the counter, the open jars and packets. Why do you assemble these absurd trays of food, why do you act as if you don't have the right to go into the living room? They're guests, this is our home, or isn't it?

Tomas did not respond, but only reached up into the cupboard to take out a box of crackers, of some variety I had never seen before in the apartment, that I myself might have liked, but that I knew Tomas must have purchased for this very moment, in anticipation of this request. I shook my head, the anger percolating through me, a series of small internal eruptions. Are you going to answer? I asked. He turned to me at last, holding a little dish replete with crackers, and said, with irritating mildness, You're overreacting. His voice was smooth and tempered—complacent in a way that was new, as if he were nursing some private delight that had already lessened his need of the world outside.

Isn't this what we always hoped for Xavier? he continued in that tranquil voice. That he would find something that he cared about, some passion? We always worried over how directionless he seemed to be, we always talked about how little ambition he seemed to have. Now look at him. He gazed at me with an expression of pleasure and pride, and I felt my frustration mount again. But what am I looking at? I asked. He spends his days lying on the sofa, he isn't writing, he's not in school, he's not doing anything in particular. I know he has his work with Anne but it isn't even clear when that will continue. Do we know that it will? Where has Anne gone? I should send her a message, I should ask when she's returning, I said and reached for my phone. Tomas gave a sharp shake of his head, and I stopped.

I set the phone down. Had it always been this way between us? Was this a familiar bone of contention, a set of roles regularly performed? Tomas the parent with the greater sympathy, the one to withhold judgment and manage expectation? And had I been the one lacking in equal restraint, too full of impulse and self-regard? Now he frowned and said, You're being too critical. He has been working very hard, you said so yourself, and he has found an area of passion if not an exact role. That is natural. He is young. He lifted his hands and placed them on my shoulders, his touch heavy as lead. This is good, he said pleadingly. This is good. I was almost persuaded, I wanted it so much to be. But as I stared up into his face, there was something unnatural in the widening of his eyes, a hint of rictus in his smile. I recalled all the times in the past when I had been comforted by Tomas, when he had told me that everything was going to be okay, and he had held me and my doubts had been assuaged. Now I could only see each of those instances as examples of capitulation, I had given in to his story, his narrative, because it had been easier, and because of his persuasiveness—persuasion, which is only one step removed from coercion.

I shook myself free and turned away from him. Once, this would have been enough, once, this would have made him come to me. But he only gave a little shrug and picked up the plate of crackers. You're not taking that in, I said. He turned and began making his way down the corridor, to the living room, to Xavier and Hana. You're not actually doing it, I said. And he called over his shoulder, You're overreacting, a little singsong lilt to his voice. There was something in his tone, it was at once absolute and condescending, and I felt a surge of anger such as I had never felt before, not toward Tomas. As he neared the living room with his plate, the thought flashed through my head, that it would take only one push for the man to come tumbling down.

And no one to put him together again. He continued forward eagerly, so that the distance between us grew, and by grace of that distance—too far for impulse to traverse—it did not happen. The hand at the back. The tangle of feet and ankle. Perhaps I would have crossed that distance, propelled by my rage, had he not stepped over the threshold and into the living room, into the space that was designated theirs, by some process that bewildered me even now, and that I would never come to understand. As he passed into the living room, I had again the terrible sense of familiarity, the knowledge that I could not place or source and therefore could not trust, so that it was not knowledge but understanding, which is not dependent on proof, and which therefore cannot be refuted—the anger, like the words, the challenge, the feeling of his insufficiency, none of it was new, all of it had taken place before.

I stopped where I was in the corridor. Through the doorway into the living room I watched as he set the plate of crackers down, not by Xavier, who had been the one to ask for them, but by Hana. And as he set the plate down by her elbow—sharp and pale like a piece of bone, washed upon the shore—I saw in his expression not the expected obsequiousness, but something else altogether, a surreptitious, shameful voracity that I recognized at once in its banality, the appreciation of an old man for a young woman. I blinked and the expression was gone, he had turned to Xavier, he seemed to be murmuring some low words of affection, in response to which Xavier reached up and took Tomas's hand. Tomas bent down to him, he said something and clapped him on the shoulder. Xavier held his father's hand and then, in a synchronized movement, they both looked up and across the living room: the double-barrel of their faces. They did not generally look alike, there was almost nothing of Tomas in Xavier, racially or otherwise, he was entirely my child, and yet as they gazed at me now, their expressions were the same, the effect like a doubling, a repetition, in which their individual selves, such as I had always known them, dissolved.

12

FOR THE NEXT FEW DAYS, AS IF SOME AGREEMENT HAD been reached between them, or as if they had been simultaneously moved by the same emotion, neither Tomas nor Xavier met me at the theater after the show. I went with the other actors to dinner, or more often with people who had come to see the play, of which there were now many, it was the final week and it was their last chance to see it. I sat alone, around those dinner tables cluttered with noise, with animation, which grew increasingly remote over the course of the meal. I listened to the requisite words of praise, and sometimes I would remember to smile graciously in response, but more often I would forget, and would sit in a distracted and unreceptive silence until the atmosphere would falter and the conversation fail.

That particular night, there were more silences than usual. I was fatigued, the countdown to the final performance was weighing heavier and heavier upon me, I could not escape the sense of the show's impending closure. It provoked a fever in me, I entered the play in a state of agitation, exploring the space in a frenetic way, unmeasured and without discipline, like an animal dragging its snout along the dirt, like an animal rubbing its back into the ground, it would only be ten more times, eight more times, five more times. I could never get enough, but I also knew that my preoccupation was a problem, that the performances were growing ragged around the edges, my sense of that finality increasingly fatal. That night, I understood that it was time to move on, that the turn had already taken place and everything would only degrade from here, I could only do this a few more times at most.

It was the force of this realization that kept me silent throughout dinner, that evening I could not rouse myself to even the minimum level of courtesy, and I could see that the others around the table—people I did not know very well, some actors and a writer, people with whom I had nothing to do—were beginning to grow uncomfortable, and that soon their discomfort would harden into dislike, they would talk about the terrible evening they had spent in my company, perhaps they would even mock me a little, my hauteur, my arrogance, I could see it already. I was holding the stem of my wineglass in my fingers, tapping the bowl of it restlessly, and now I carefully knocked the glass over, so that a stain blossomed on the tablecloth, and the others startled and pushed back their chairs. I apologized and said that I must have been more tired than I realized, I dabbed ineffectually at the spill until the waiter appeared and began to move the plates and glasses in order to change the cloth, I continued to apologize, and then it seemed very natural, entirely acceptable for me to excuse myself. The others rose to their feet, faces sympathetic, and this time when they reiterated their words of praise they seemed to me a little more sincere, brightened as they were by the promise of my departure, and I was able to respond in a manner that would, I knew, ensure that they would leave with the impression that I was not so bad after all.

I left the restaurant in a state of considerable relief, in the giddy rush of having extracted myself from that interminable dinner, the feeling was delicious. I walked briskly, and when I reached the apartment, I checked the time and saw that it was still early. I decided to walk around a block or two, to enjoy the sensation of warm air on my skin, winter had at last come to an end and I was not ready to go inside.

As I turned the corner, I happened to look back at our building from across the street, things would have turned out very differently had I not done so. My gaze moved up and then up again, until it found our floor and our apartment. Every window was brightly illuminated, a series of vivid rectangles across the living room and kitchen and bedrooms, even the small room at the back, Tomas's study, in which he always worked by the light of his desk lamp, and never with the ceiling light switched on—even that room burned with light.

I frowned, at first I did not understand what I was seeing. It was our apartment, I knew that it was our apartment, but it was grossly transformed. Vertigo slowly took hold, its grip an asphyxiation. Something was very wrong. I turned and went to the front of the building, running along the length of the street, so that I was out of breath when I reached the entrance and slammed into the glass door, pushing it open. I was at the elevator before the front door had closed, the outside air gusting into the lobby and then slowly dissipating, I pressed my thumb into the up button with senseless haste, the elevator would not come faster, no matter how many times I pressed the button, and yet—

I imagined: an accident, a seizure, the howl of an ambulance descending. At last, the elevator arrived and as it crawled up the floors of the building, the movement so slow it was agony, I leaned my head back and tried to breathe, there were exercises I had been taught for situations like these, there were things I had been told to do. Perhaps it would be okay, perhaps it was not as it appeared, and then I had the sudden and infantile wish to stay in the quiet of the elevator, a bird with its head in the sand, if I could stay here forever, if I could remain in this tightly enclosed space, then I would be safe, we would all be safe. But then the familiar chime as the doors opened and I felt the vertigo seize me again. I stumbled out into the corridor and I opened the door to the apartment.

Inside, too much light, every lamp and fixture switched on, so that the interior appeared strangely flattened, without the depth of a normal room. The objects in the apartment looked suddenly insubstantial, almost like props, of the sort that appeared a perfect likeness but revealed themselves to be falsely constructed when you handled them, too light, or only partially composed. I leaned against the wall to steady myself, and discovered that it too seemed hollow, thin and rickety, as if it might collapse if I leaned with too much weight. The walls of my very own home, the apartment I had lived in for so long. From the far end of the corridor I heard a thump, and then a second thump, and then a third thump, and I hurried in its direction to the living room, where all the lights were blazing.

I saw Xavier first, patrolling the room, holding a throw pillow in one hand and smacking it with the palm of the other, making that thumping sound, that terrible thumping sound. I stared at him as he stalked round and round. It was as if there had been a secret self he had kept hidden inside, the shadow of which I had distantly perceived, and now at last he had released it. Come out, come out, he said in a voice I had never heard before, a high whistle that menaced like a growl. His movements were spiky and exaggerated as he swiveled his head from side to side, goose-stepping across the carpet and smacking the pillow again.

I looked around the room, fear mounting inside me. The tables were covered in empty bottles and on the floor was a fallen glass, a blotch of red vivid upon the carpet. Suddenly, Tomas emerged from behind the sofa, crawling on all fours. Not here! he called out in a strangely chipper voice, like a cadet reporting for duty, or a child at school attendance, although it was *not here* rather than *here*. They were conducting a search of some kind, a raid. Not here! he repeated and my breath caught, there was something grotesque about the sight of Tomas on the floor, head lolling heavy from his neck, Tomas who had always relied so much upon dignity in the composition of his self-image, in the self that he presented to the world, to me.

What is this? I said loudly and they both turned. The pillow dropped from Xavier's hand and fell softly to the floor. Tomas scrambled awkwardly to his feet—I felt the ache in his back, in his knees, I felt the agedness of his body. I looked around the room again, apart from the bottles and glasses, the surfaces were empty, the clutter removed. The desk, for example, that monstrosity ranged along the wall, it had been cleared and was now completely bare. Where is Hana? I asked sharply. The room was devoid of her presence, the sweaters and books and papers that were hers, that I had folded and tidied numerous times, they too were gone. What has happened? I said to Tomas and Xavier, they looked like little children, their faces ringed with guilt. Where is Hana? I repeated.

She's out, Xavier whispered, and hung his head. What do you mean by out? I asked. All her things are gone. Has she found somewhere else to stay? Xavier shook his head, as if he himself did not know her whereabouts or the answer, he licked his lips and finally said, She's not here. She could be back as soon as tomorrow, or the day after, but for the time being she is not here. I turned to Tomas, who would not look at me either, and I took an involuntary step forward. What have you been doing? I said. What has been taking place in here? There was a sound, from the other side of the apartment, and I looked up sharply. Nothing, Tomas said faintly, as Xavier's entire face lit up. He let out a triumphant cry and galloped across the room and disappeared down the corridor. It was just a game, Tomas said weakly. Just a game.

There was another thump and then the high-pitched squeal of Hana's laughter shot toward us. Tomas gave a start, a little twitch that ran through his body, he remained still for a second and then another, he closed his eyes, his body vibrating with tension, one foot shuffling surreptitiously along the floor, until he could no longer contain himself and with a yelp he scuttled out the living room and after Xavier. I turned and followed, they had gone into Tomas's study. From my end of the corridor, as if staring down the wrong end of a telescope, I saw Hana tumbling out of a closet, lying on the floor, all three screeching with laughter, Tomas almost doubling over with mirth as Xavier helped Hana to her feet.

Rigid, I watched from where I stood, at the far end of the corridor, which now appeared longer than usual, which seemed mysteriously to have extended, the three of them appearing to me as in a tableau, Hana prone on the ground, Xavier kneeling to help her, Tomas hovering over them like some worried supplicant, or fretful court jester, or malevolent spirit. It was Tomas, there was something in the sight of him that was impossible, an image that I could not begin to process, and that kept me from going to them, even as I knew I should. Hana continued to laugh, as Xavier lifted her by her arms in an ungainly and cavalier fashion, the way he was touching her was rough and brusque and she slipped from his grasp and fell to the ground again, still laughing.

Now Tomas kneeled to help her and I watched as his hand wrapped around the tender flesh of her arm, as the other hand snaked around her torso, higher than her waist, so that the grasp of his fingers was around her breast. He wore an expression of cautious avidity, like a man who had been biding his time, waiting for the right moment, believing and also not daring to believe it had come at last. The glazed expression of lust in his eyes, the contrapuntal scurrying and squeezing of his hand. I had never seen his face so devoid of familiarity, as if he were a vessel that had been upended, everything that made him himself trickling to the floor.

At that moment, her breast in my husband's hand, Hana slid her gaze over to me and stared, from across the distance of that long corridor. There was no shame or embarrassment in her eyes, instead they glinted with amusement and triumph. She gave a vicious little slap at Tomas's hand. Naughty! Naughty! she screamed. Dirty old man! And then she began laughing to show that she did not mean it, she threw her head back to say that it was only in good fun, I might have done the same myself, once upon a time. Amidst the violent tumble in my head, I felt a stab of surprise, how could it be, that a woman of her age and generation, how could it be that she would still feel the need to do such things?

At the sound of her screaming, Xavier turned to look at Hana and then at Tomas. Together, we watched as she wrapped her arms around Tomas, the two of them in that obscene embrace. From where I stood, I could see Xavier begin to tremble, his shoulders hunching forward, and I understood that he was now in distress. He turned, with a wandering movement of the head, and I knew that he was looking for me. His gaze found me and for a long moment we stared at each other. There was a demand in his face, the demand of a child, asking his mother to make an intolerable situation better. I remained frozen at the far end of the corridor, I saw his face in all its vulnerability, the fear of disappointment dawning in his features, and I realized that he was waiting for me.

It is no small thing to realize that you are the one who is waited for, and it is also the perpetual condition of motherhood, the waiting never stops. And so it was, it was because of this, that I made my way down the corridor, it was for Xavier. I hurried to him, carrying my heart inside my mouth, I went as fast as I possibly could, but even as I approached I could see the bond between us grow slack, and by the time I reached them, the open door of his expectation had already begun to swing shut, another moment and it had closed. And I was left outside. And it was because of this that I behaved, I knew I was behaving, badly. As if another person slipped inside me, another woman altogether.

I did not go to Xavier. Instead, I wrenched Tomas to his feet with more force than I thought I had in my body, you hear stories about women who perform extraordinary feats of strength when their child is in danger, lifting a car or some such, what did it mean, that I found such strength in a moment of outrage? I pulled him up so that he tripped and fell hard against the wall, his dear and aged head bouncing off its surface, almost as if I had pushed him there, almost as if I had flung him to the floor, although such a thing wasn't possible, and couldn't be real. Xavier gave a cry of alarm and went to him at once, but I did not, instead I pulled Hana to her feet and began dragging her to the front door.

She followed me without protest, her body floating alongside me as we made our way down the corridor, bizarrely insubstantial, she who had exerted such corporeal force upon us only seconds earlier, now she moved alongside me with so little resistance she might have been a ghost, and when we reached the front door she opened it herself and stepped through without protest, as if she had been expecting it, as if she had been waiting for this moment, which I now understood had long been inevitable. She turned only when she was outside the apartment, and I saw—I saw in her face an expression that could only be described as pity. She turned away very quickly, as if to remove her face from mine, and I understood then that she had not intended for me to see her expression, that it was a pure and unguarded response to me, as I was in that moment.

An instant later, she was gone. The door swung closed and I stared after her in bewilderment, I couldn't understand what had taken place. The emptiness that she left behind gaped before me. From the other end of the apartment, I heard Xavier groan. Has she gone? Did you let her go? He rose and came staggering in my direction. What did you say to her? he shouted. I said nothing, I told him, I said nothing. But he shook his head as if this could not be possible and began to fumble at the door as I repeated, I said nothing, and as he flung the door open and looked down the hallway for her, as he lunged for the elevator, and then the stairs, I called after him, She said nothing, she went without a word. You see, she knew she needed to go. He disappeared down the stairs with a clatter before I could stop him, although it is also true that I did not try, not as hard as I could have, instead I turned and ran to Tomas.

He was sitting up and I slowed to a stop before him. We stared at each other, as if neither of us was willing or able to make the first move. Then he reached his hand out. I sat down beside him without taking it. He gave a long exhalation and lowered his hand. His fingers tapped restlessly on his leg and then I reached for his hand, if only to stop that movement, I held it as tightly as I could. He turned his head, still resting it against the wall, as if he could not yet hold it up. He asked if she was gone. I nodded. He was very still. Well, he said, and I nodded again and gripped his hand tighter in mine. As I did so, Xavier came pounding into the apartment, down the corridor, and slowly we got to our feet, as if we knew that the moment of confrontation had come.

Xavier stood before us, breathing heavily. It had to end, I said firmly. You know this, the arrangement was impossible. And Xavier replied, It was impossible because of you, because you're fucking crazy, *Mom*, you're fucking crazy. His voice, its delivery, it was as if the word *Mom* were in quotation marks, as if it did not refer to the thing itself but its inverse. The word *Mom*, reverberating through the room, clanging around inside my head. Before me, his face slipped away piece by piece, until I saw nothing of myself in him, nothing at all. You're no son of mine, I said, and he laughed. How could I be? Just look at yourself. The words heavy with contempt. I heard Tomas's voice as if from a great distance, Don't speak to your mother that way, and he stepped forward as if to push Xavier away but his arms were weak and the gesture ineffectual, Xavier merely gave a bitter laugh and stepped to one side to avoid him. What do you want from me? I asked and Xavier laughed again. Please, Tomas said, You should go.

Xavier said, I'm going, I'll call you, he said this to Tomas. And then as he turned away, as we followed him down the corridor and into the living room, I thought no, I said no. I clapped my hands together once, the sound explosive in the room. I saw Xavier give a start, as one would do at the sound of a car backfiring, or a gunshot ringing through the street. His shoulders raised, his back curved, I thought he might cover his ears with his hands. He was staring down at the floor, he would not turn to look at me. When I spoke, it was with all the finality I did not feel, I spoke as if the words were an incantation of sorts. I said, It's over. And although neither Xavier nor Tomas moved, instantly the space had transformed, so that we were no longer a family standing in a room—a family with problems, with dramas and resentments and everything else, but still a family—and instead three distinct people, atomized, standing in a room suddenly devoid of meaning.

Xavier looked up, not at me but at Tomas, and I saw that there was a question in his eyes. I looked across at Tomas and I knew he was not convinced, that some part of him wished to stay inside the performance, inside the fantasy, I could see the thought moving through his head and nearly settling, what was a family if not a shared delusion, a mutual construction? And equally I saw that Xavier believed that if he could persuade Tomas, then it would be the two of them, two of three, a majority that could sustain the fantasy we had agreed to live inside. But he was wrong, he overestimated his powers of persuasion, the record of these past weeks. I had years, I had an entire lifetime, to wield over Tomas, and I knew that he would not leave me, not in this regard nor in any other.

In the end, it was Xavier who stepped outside the circle first, perhaps because he quickly accepted what I already knew, so that it was Tomas who remained inside, alone. I stared at him and thought I had never seen him appear quite so forlorn. He seemed to gesture out to us—as if to say, were we both so certain, as if to beseech us to step inside the enchanted circle again. But it was too late, the room had already transformed, it was just a room in an apartment in a city, it was just a couple and a stranger, a person whose presence they no longer fully understood, the group had already cleaved into us and him, and Xavier, sensing this at once, was not going to wait for Tomas to deliver the fatal blow. Tomas, slow-moving as ever.

Xavier made a sound, difficult to describe, somewhere between a moan and an exhalation, a high-pitched laugh. He began to gather his things from around the living room, as Hana must have done not too many hours earlier, he disappeared into the bedroom and returned with a duffel bag, into which he stuffed his books and his clothes, I realized how thoroughly they had decamped into the living room. It couldn't last, he said as he collected his things. He zipped his bag, he turned to look at us. But what if it had? Tomas moved his hands helplessly through the air and when he looked at Xavier, it was with tremendous tenderness and longing. What will you do? he asked, voice trembling. Xavier said nothing. He only shook his head, and was gone.

13

AND THEN I LEARNED HOW QUIET THE APARTMENT RE-
ally could be, hushed as it now was with remorse and disappointment. I wondered, as I stood in the silence that
extended into days and into weeks, what I had done. It was
as though I had been embraced by a passing madness. I
looked at Tomas and I tried to remember, I tried to return
to that state of frenzied conviction, I had been enervated, and
excited, but now there was only regret, pooling inside me.

As for Xavier, I no longer knew what he was to me, or
what I was to him. We had been playing parts, and for a
period—for as long as we understood our roles, for as long
as we participated in the careful collusion that is a story, that

is a family, told by one person to another person—the mechanism had held. But the deeper the complicity, and the longer it is sustained, the less give there is, the more binding and unforgiving the contract, and in the end it took very little for the whole thing to collapse. It was as if a break had been called, as if it had suddenly occurred to both of us that his lines were insufficient, my characterization lacking, the entire plotline faulty and implausible.

Or perhaps he was only acting out. Perhaps it was only that, and less than I thought it was. Can things be unsaid and undone, can the clock run both ways, backward and forward, can the story unspool in both directions? Some days later, I returned home to find that all his things had gone, I assumed that Tomas had arranged their removal. I understood that the two of them were in contact. I didn't expect Tomas to give him up. I didn't even want him to. In the desolate apartment, I was dimly reassured by the vibration of his phone, at breakfast or in the middle of the night, to know that some channel of communication remained open, that Xavier was, at least, safe. I felt increasingly ashamed of what had taken place. It was not only the confrontation, it was everything that had preceded it, we had revealed ourselves more than we intended, we had exchanged the blueprint of our most private desires in a way that was near indecent.

The play closed. Those final performances were empty, I was only going through the motions, everyone around me and in the audience could tell. I had wrung the thing dry. And yet when it was over, I still felt its absence. The apartment grew bigger, it grew emptier. Of course, I wondered about Xavier. As long as Tomas and Xavier were in touch, as long as they were speaking, by whatever modes and registers were available to them, the possibility remained—not of a reconciliation, but of a reconstitution. A recommencement. Is such a thing possible? I asked Tomas. He was silent. I wondered if he understood what I was asking. But of course he did, he understood everything. He always did. That was the thing about Tomas.

One month later, Xavier returned to the apartment. Before Tomas opened the door, I wondered who would appear, which version of him would be waiting, which person I would see. Perhaps Xavier wondered the same of me. But it was Tomas who opened the door, and so it was Tomas he saw first, and when they embraced it seemed both natural and inevitable, there was no awkwardness between them, no strain or animosity.

But when he turned to me, Xavier seemed to shrink

away—and I felt a pang, it was not only that he would cower from me, it was the fact that there was something in the movement that was not entirely specific, so that he could have been shrinking away from anyone, I was no longer any person in particular to him. I took his hand in both of mine, but I was not able to embrace him in the way that Tomas had, I was aware that I was able to give less than perhaps he wanted, less certainly than I wished. I released his hand and asked him to come into the living room and we all paused at my words, I had spoken to him as if he were only a visitor here, as if he were a stranger. But perhaps he was both those things. In any case, it was only a brief moment before he nodded and followed me.

We sat down on the sofas so that we were facing one another, as if to maximize the distance between us, and it was only when I looked at him from across that stretch of space that I could interpret his affect, at once sullen but also prideful and excited. He rose to his feet again and extracted a bundle of folded pages from the pocket of his coat. He hesitated, and then held out the papers to Tomas. Still, it was clear the gesture was directed at me, so that we knew, all three of us, that the message contained in those creased pieces of paper was addressed not to Tomas, but to me.

Tomas glanced in my direction. He did not move or take the papers. Xavier gave a little shrug and then placed the bundle on the corner of the coffee table. He sat back down on the sofa. Only then did Tomas lean forward. He brought his hand to the papers, palm hovering over the pages, fingers outstretched. What is it? he asked Xavier, and I could already hear the curiosity beneath the thin layer of trepidation. The curiosity instantly deepened, perhaps was tempered with relief, when Xavier replied, A play. At which point I raised my head to find they had both turned toward me, or perhaps Xavier had been watching me the entire time.

I looked over at the desk beneath the windows, the desk that Tomas had bought for Xavier not so very long ago, and that now sat with its surface bare and gleaming, and I realized that I had been wrong about one thing at least, all that time it had not been Hana who had been working, but Xavier. Despite all appearances to the contrary, Xavier lying on the sofa, on the floor, Xavier flipping idly through a book or magazine, I knew from the manner of presentation, from the way he told Tomas that he had something he wanted to share with us, even from the way he set the little pile of papers down on the table, I knew that it was Xavier's work alone, all of it, every last word.

Tomas cleared his throat and said, So you finished it. His fingers brushed the surface of the pages almost tenderly. He picked up the manuscript and I knew that he was intrigued, that he could not wait to begin reading it, and that in some way this was the culmination of a long-suppressed hope he hadn't wholly realized he was harboring. He gazed at Xavier with pride—pride in and through another person. He was transformed by the breadth of his emotion, stepping outside himself and extending the boundaries of his being, and I knew that this was one definition of love.

I wanted nothing more than for Tomas to stay inside the container of this feeling, which I could see growing with each passing second—this was what I wanted for him. But he only lowered his head and was silent. What kind of play? I asked at last and Xavier looked at me. His gaze was steady and clear, and for the first time I had a sense of the consistency of his ego, and I knew that he was someone who could make a piece of work, many of them perhaps. No, I had not understood him correctly at all. He replied, A monologue. And the next question rushed out of me before I could stop it. What kind of part? He nodded as if he had expected the question, and I knew he had heard the greed in my voice, just as I myself had heard it. A woman of your age and general disposition, he said. A woman who can no longer distinguish between what is real and what is not real.

We gazed at each other. I waited to see if his face would loosen and duck back into its habitual evasion, if he would once more become his old self. But instead, I felt the renewed force of his ego as it pushed its way forward, he had changed past the point of recognition. He had become him-self. I gave a short laugh. Isn't that a little on the nose? I said, and got to my feet. What should I do with this? Tomas asked Xavier. I wondered why he asked, when it was it per-fectly obvious what Xavier wanted. He wants you to read it, I said sharply from the doorway. He wants to know what you think.

But Tomas shook his head, and then he said to Xavier in a perfectly reasonable voice, in a gentle voice, Who would you like to read it first? I imagine it is not me. I imagine this is written for—and he turned to me, and for the briefest of moments, I saw the grasp of his hand tighten on the pages. Then he offered them to me, fingers already slackening. I imagine this is for you. And he gave a little swallow as he continued to hold the manuscript out to me, and I under-stood that it wasn't easy for him, that he was relinquishing something too. I looked at Xavier, at his face trying to con-ceal its hope, I looked at Tomas's hand extended toward me, and I came back into the room.

Here, it is possible to be two things at once. Not a splitting of personality or psyche, but the natural superimposition of one mind on top of another mind. In the space between them, a performance becomes possible. You observe your-self, you watch yourself act, you hear yourself speak, a line that is articulated and then articulated again, and the mean-ing that is produced is at once entirely real—as it is experi-enced on stage, as it is experienced by the audience—and also the predictable result of your craft, the choices you have made, the control that cedes freedom.

I stand on the stage. I look out into the audience, which is full, the kind of house that Xavier must have dreamed of, possibly from the very start. Xavier, whose ambition has the depth and power of my own. It is the kind of house I myself wanted in the early days of my career, when the au-dience and its recognition was all I seemed to seek. Always to be seen, in those days it was almost an end in itself, be-cause it was in being seen that I could say for certain that I existed, that my limbs were real as I touched them, that my being was intact as it peered out into the world. A stay against the turbulence within me—that was, perhaps, the purpose of all this.

I know that Xavier is seeking the same thing, and it is possible he has already found it. To know that he exists to the world, and in the world, in a continual sequence of rec-ognition. But such things do not last, not in the way that he thinks. The recognition comes and goes, too many parts—those onstage and in life—don't endure, and once they are gone, their logic is impossible to regain. Mostly, there is only the emptiness they leave behind. But this is not something that I will say to him. This is something he must discover for himself. Instead, I stand on this stage, in the story he has created, in the role he has made. Before me—a face or two that I can pick out in the crowd. A chain of words, sturdy as a cable, a voice that has been given to me. And around me the waiting darkness.

ACKNOWLEDGMENTS

My gratitude to Ellen Levine, Rebecca Saletan, Laura Percia-sepe, Jynne Dilling Martin, Geoff Kloske, Ashley Garland, Claire McGinnis, Glory Anne Plata, Kitanna Hiromasa, Nora Alice Demick, Michelle Waters, Viviann Do, Helen Yentus, Lauren Peters-Collaer, Delia Taylor, Sharon Gonzalez, and everyone at Riverhead and Trident Media. In the UK, my thanks to Clare Conville, Michal Shavit, Sean Hayes, Alex Russell, and all at Fern Press and Conville and Walsh.

Large portions of this book were written while in residence at the Jan Michalski Foundation and Shakespeare and Company Bookstore; I completed the manuscript as a Rome Prize Fellow in Literature at the American Academy in Rome. I am grateful to these institutions and the extraordinary people who run them for their generosity, imagination, and support.

Finally, as always, my love to Hari, Ryu, and Mila, without whom none of this would be possible.